Lucy
Unstrung

Carole Lazar

Tundra Books

Published in Canada by Tundra Books,
75 Sherbourne Street, Toronto, Ontario M5A 2P9

Published in the United States by Tundra Books of Northern New York,
P.O. Box 1030, Plattsburgh, New York 12901

Library of Congress Control Number: 2009938447

Library and Archives Canada Cataloguing in Publication

Lazar, Carole
Lucy unstrung / Carole Lazar.

ISBN 978-0-88776-963-4

I. Title.

PS8623.A949L83 2010   jC813'.6   C2009-905863-4

We acknowledge the financial support of the Government of Canada
through the Book Publishing Industry Development Program (BPIDP) and
that of the Government of Ontario through the Ontario Media Development Corporation's Ontario Book Initiative. We further acknowledge the
support of the Canada Council for the Arts and the Ontario Arts Council
for our publishing program.

ONTARIO ARTS COUNCIL
CONSEIL DES ARTS DE L'ONTARIO

Design: Kelly Hill

Printed and bound in Canada

1 2 3 4 5 6   15 14 13 12 11 10

To my daughter, Susan.
You were always on my mind.

one

When my mom finally walks in the door at nine-fifteen, she acts like nothing's wrong at all.

"Where have you been?" I ask. "Dad and I have been worried sick. And now Grandma's upset too."

"What are you talking about? You knew I was going to my pilates class. What's Grandma upset about?"

"We were worried because it's dark out and no one knew where you were."

It's me who's doing the talking, but Mom looks right past me and glares at Dad.

"Who called my mother?"

"I thought you might have dropped in there," he says. "You were later than you usually are."

"You wouldn't like it if I got home this late," I say.

"Maybe that's because you're only thirteen. I'm twenty-eight. There's supposed to be a difference."

"I don't see why. Grandma always tells me it's important to be dependable. If you aren't and no one knows when you're going to show up, you could get raped, murdered, and thrown into a ditch, and your family would just think you were late again. No one would even call the police."

"Like I could be so lucky," she says.

"I just got worried when you weren't home by nine o'clock," Dad says. "I mean, the gym is only a five-minute drive from here and I knew the class was over at eight. I allowed twenty minutes for you to shower and change . . ."

"Gina and I went to Starbucks for a coffee. So call the cops, get together a search party, or just shoot me – I don't care! But don't call my mother!"

"Starbucks?" Dad says. "What did you have?"

"Coffee. Just a regular coffee."

"They call it a *tall*, I think."

"Who cares what they call it?"

Mom is raising her voice again. I don't know why she gets all twisted out of shape about Dad making a simple observation like that.

"You know," he says. "The tall at Starbucks is twelve ounces and it's expensive. You can get a sixteen-ounce coffee at McDonald's or A&W for just over a dollar."

"What did I do to deserve this?" my mom wails.

"Grandma says it's always better to bring friends home, and I bet it would be even cheaper if you'd waited till you got back here to have coffee," I say.

"One little mistake when I'm fourteen and my whole life is ruined. I don't know what's worse: being married to a walking spreadsheet or being doomed to live with a doppelgänger of my mother."

"What's a doppelgänger?"

"Look it up in the dictionary," she says.

I want to tell her it would be much faster if she'd just tell me herself, but she goes stomping out of the kitchen and heads upstairs.

I get the dictionary.

"How would you spell that?" I ask Dad.

"Pretty much the way it sounds," Dad says. "*D-o-p-p-e-l-g-a-n-g-e-r.*"

I find the word. It means a ghostly likeness or double of a living person.

Dad is back at the computer, where he's entering the money Mom spent on the coffee in to an accounting program he uses to keep track of all our finances. Once a week, he prints out a copy so he and Mom can discuss money. The printout is called a spreadsheet. I think my mom was calling Dad a walking spreadsheet because he hardly needs this software to keep track of spending. He could probably keep it all in his head. He has a very good memory for figures.

"Why did she call me a double of Grandma?" I ask. "I don't think we look anything alike."

Dad looks up at me from the computer screen. "No, Lucy, I don't think that's what she meant. It's just that you quote your grandma so much that sometimes it feels like she's living here. You know how your mom and grandma tend to lock horns now and then. I think it upsets her when you remind her of what your grandma would say all the time."

It isn't until later, when I'm in bed, that I start wondering if she really meant what she said about how a mistake she made when she was fourteen – getting pregnant with me – has wrecked her life. My mother was fifteen when I was born. She got pregnant in Grade 9 because there were no Catholic high schools in Surrey in those days, and she had to go to a public school. My mom was very innocent and unworldly, and the supervision at that high school just wasn't what it should have been. Grandma explained that part to me. My mother says that her class went on a ski trip to Mt. Seymour. She'd never been skiing before and her clothes weren't warm enough. By lunchtime, she was shivering with cold. One of the ski instructors, a handsome exchange student from Sweden, felt sorry for her. He invited her to come and sit in his car. He said he'd turn the heater on and it would be way warmer than the drafty old lodge where everyone else was having lunch. Mom says his English wasn't very good and that she had trouble understanding him. She never really gets much beyond that in her explanation. Even if his English was bad and she was innocent, unworldly, and very cold, you'd think she might have clued in at least in time to avoid getting pregnant.

I imagine it was a bit of a shock when my mom, my grandparents, and finally everyone in the neighborhood, the school, and our parish discovered that I was on the way. But it all turned out okay. Her life's not ruined. Still, when she said those words, it made me feel kind of guilty. Maybe it's because I'm Catholic.

If you're Catholic, you don't have to actually *do* anything to be guilty. We believe in original sin. It all goes back to Adam and Eve. When they ate that apple, they brought sin into the world, so now we inherit sin along with our DNA. That's why we baptize babies. Baptism washes away this original sin. But that isn't the end of it. Even after baptism, the tendency to be willful and disobedient clings like an old habit. I imagine it's like smoking or biting your nails: really hard to break. Watch any two year old having a tantrum in the supermarket. You just know that when God finished making people and, the Bible says, "He saw that it was good," this wasn't at all what He had in mind.

I'm lying there thinking about it when Dad sticks his head into my room to ask if he can borrow my extra pillow. For some reason, he's decided to sleep on the couch.

"Do you think Mom meant it when she said I wrecked her life?" I ask.

"No, of course not," he says. "She's just blowing off steam."

I think he's probably right, so I don't think too much more about it just then. It isn't until later, when she starts wrecking *my* life, that I realize maybe she did mean it, and she's just been waiting all these years for a chance to seek revenge.

two

It starts first thing in the morning. How am I supposed to sleep with her vacuuming right outside my bedroom door? I cover my head with my pillow. The next thing I know, she's yanking my blankets off.

"Come on, Lucy. It's time to get up. I've got plans today."

I try to pull the blankets back up. "Who cares?" I'm still sleepy. "It's hard on a kid when parents fight all night, you know."

"It's been eleven hours since anyone said a word in this house," she says. "Get up. I want to get these sheets in the wash."

I swing my feet over the side of the bed and she kicks my slippers toward me. She's already pulling at my sheets, and if I don't get off the bed, she'll probably pull me onto the floor when she gives them that final tug.

I get up and start for the door.

"Take these down to the laundry room," she says.

"Why should I have to do everything just because you're in a bad mood?"

"You think I'm in a bad mood? You've seen nothing! Don't give me any more grief or I'll show you what a bad mood really looks like." She flings the sheets at me. "Take your laundry basket too."

If looks could kill, my mother would be dead; I am so mad at her. But she doesn't even see me. She's busy making up my bed with clean sheets.

I stomp downstairs and throw the laundry basket onto the floor next to the washer. It tips onto its side and some of the clothes spill out. I don't care.

I head for the kitchen. There's absolutely no sign of breakfast. The coffeepot is empty, the toaster's been put away, and I notice there are places on the floor that are still wet from mopping. She's cleaned up the kitchen without even thinking about me or the fact that I just might want something to eat. The weekend paper is on the table, so I grab the Life section, which is my favorite one. I can hear my mom vacuuming again. I wish she'd hurry up.

She doesn't usually stay mad so long. Grandma always tells Dad and me just to ignore Mom's bad moods. Usually that works fine. She gets over them and everything goes back to normal until the next time something sets her off.

I hear the thump of the vacuum as she pulls it down a step or two on the stairs. It would be easier for her if we had a built-in system. They are much quieter, so she could vacuum without waking me up. Her birthday is coming up in a couple of months. I'll talk to Dad about it.

I wander out to the hall and watch as she finishes the stairs and hauls our old canister vacuum to the closet in the laundry room.

"Where's Dad?" I ask.

"He took the van in for servicing."

"What's for breakfast?"

"I had half a bagel with peanut butter," she says.

"But what am I supposed to have?"

"You can have the other half, if you want."

She's not really paying attention to me. She's started sorting laundry as if I'm not even there.

"But I don't want a bagel."

"Well, go find something you do want then."

"Aren't you going to fix anything for me?"

She stops what she's doing and turns to face me. "What is it you'd like?"

"Just cereal. Oh, and maybe some juice."

"Do you know where the cereal is?"

"Of course."

"Do you think you could be very grown up and pour some in a bowl for yourself?"

I'm about to tell her I don't appreciate her sarcasm when the phone rings.

"I bet that's Grandma," I say. "She's probably wondering if you ever did come home."

"I phoned your grandma last night. I don't think she'll be calling back any time real soon."

Mom walks into the kitchen and grabs the phone. I can tell almost as soon as she picks it up that it's Gina. Mom always sounds different when she talks to Gina. For one thing, she starts complaining right away, saying that she can't wait to get out of this house.

Mom met Gina at her pilates class. It was before Christmas, maybe four months ago. Since then, they've been seeing way too much of each other. I listen to Mom's side of the conversation. It sounds like the "plans" that were her excuse for waking me from a sound sleep involve going somewhere with Gina. Why am I not surprised?

"Where are you going? Can I come?" I ask as soon as she hangs up.

"If you don't even know where I'm going, what makes you think you'd want to come?"

"Well, I might."

"Well, you can't. It wouldn't be interesting for you. Gina and I are just going to drive around to some stores to see if we can find some packing boxes for her."

"She's moving?"

Maybe this is good news, even if I can't go with them.

"Yes, she's selling her apartment and moving in with Ian."

"But they aren't married!"

"Get used to it. It's called the real world."

"Grandma would have a heart attack if she heard you say that!"

"She didn't hear me say that, did she? So if you don't go tattling, she should live."

No one listening to my mom talk like this would ever guess that she works at Cenacle Heights Convent. You'd think that with her spending so much time with all those holy old nuns, some of the good influence would rub off on her. It probably would if she wasn't hanging around with Gina and picking up all these bad attitudes.

Gina is even older than my mom, but the trouble with her is that she has no responsibilities. She must have a job of some kind, but after work, all she does is go to pilates classes and go out for coffee. On weekends, she goes to clubs and parties. I know this because once Gina showed Mom and me some pictures and there was one of her and Ian at a nightclub. She had on this low-cut red dress that showed way more of her boobs than was proper, and she was sitting on Ian's lap. If Grandma had seen it, she'd have said Gina looked like a floozy. My mother's not that type at all. Until she met Gina, she used to spend all her evenings at home with me and Dad. She reads a lot. We all do.

Mom and I are still standing there by the phone when I hear my dad let himself in the door that comes from the garage.

"Kate," he calls. "I need your car keys."

"Why?"

"I'm taking your car in for servicing."

"You didn't tell me you'd made an appointment."

"Didn't I? It must have slipped my mind."

"It doesn't matter," she says. "I'll take the van. We can use the extra room. I'm helping Gina find moving boxes."

"I left the van at the shop."

"How did you get home?"

"One of the boys who works at the mechanic's gave me a lift."

"So you're telling me both vehicles will be at the service station all morning?"

She's not yelling or anything, but her lips are tight and thin.

"That's how I planned it, yeah. It's more efficient to do them both at the same time. Otherwise I'm left hanging around down there for two mornings."

"Wonderful!" Mom says. "And of course you never considered the possibility that I might have plans of my own?"

"Well, you don't usually go anywhere Saturday mornings," he says. "You didn't mention going out . . ."

"Mom," I interrupt him, "Why can't you just use Gina's car?"

"Thank you so much for that suggestion, Lucy. Why didn't I think of that?"

I don't know why she didn't – probably because she was looking for some excuse to start another fight.

She digs around in her purse. When she finds her keys, she flings them at Dad and storms off. She takes the phone with her.

I follow her upstairs. She goes into her room but doesn't close the door. She leans against the dresser and punches in a number. I just stand there in the doorway, watching her.

"Gina, you're going to have to come and get me. I'm not allowed to have my car today." She's quiet for a minute and then she says, "You can leave her here with Lucy."

I'm startled. I come into the room and start waving my arms around. Excuse me! Who's she leaving with me? Don't I even get consulted? I don't want to stay here with a total stranger. I'm not the kind of person who makes friends easily.

"Sure," she says. "See you in half an hour then." She hangs up.

I'm bursting. "Who are you leaving with me?"

"Lucy," she answers.

This makes no sense.

"Lucy is Gina's dog. You'll like her."

"Gina named her dog Lucy?"

"Yes, funny coincidence, isn't it?"

"What sort of a name is that for a dog?"

"I don't think it's that unusual," she says.

"But Lucy's a people name. Dogs should have dog names like Fido, or Buster, or Rover, or King . . . There are lots of good dog names."

"Those are all names for male dogs. Lucy's a female."

My mind goes blank. I can't think of any girl dog names. "But Dad's at the garage. I thought you'd drop me off at Grandma's. I don't want to be all alone here."

"You won't be. Lucy will keep you company."

"But I don't know anything about dogs."

"What's to know? She'll probably sleep most of the time. A bunch of realtors are going through Gina's apartment today, and she's afraid that having all those strangers there will upset Lucy."

"Why don't you take her with you?"

"If she's left alone in the car, she chews things."

"If you leave her here, I'll be the thing she chews. Dogs hate me. I told you about how that one in the house at the end of the cul-de-sac attacked me. I can't even go down to that end of the street now."

"What are you talking about? You've never been bitten by a dog."

"No, but he tried. He barked like he'd lost his mind, and then he slammed into the fence so hard that I thought it would break and he'd come right through it."

"Sounds very dramatic," Mom says. "That would be that high fence with the solid panels, wouldn't it?"

"Yeah."

"So you didn't actually see the dog."

"No, but . . ."

"Anyway, you don't have to worry about Lucy crashing through any fences. She's just a wee bit of a thing. Trust me. You two will get along fine."

I'm not convinced. I'm still worrying about it when the doorbell rings and Gina walks in without waiting for anyone to answer. She does this all the time. She just barges in like she owns the place. But today I have more to be concerned about than her bad manners.

I'm looking at her dog. I thought it would be something like a poodle or one of those little mop dogs. It's not.

She has long, soft, reddish-blonde-colored fur that parts in the middle of her back and sweeps down her sides, straight as can be. It's layered a bit toward the ends. It looks more like human hair than like fur. As a matter of fact, it looks just like my hair. Mine is the same color and it's parted in the middle too. My hair's so fine and straight that hairdressers always layer the ends to give it a bit of a lift. The dog is small like my mom said, but she's slimmer than I was expecting. I'm small too, and on the skinny side.

I look closely at her. She has fine features and eyes that are almost too big for her face. That's what they say about me too. Her eyes are brown. Mine are hazel. If she were human, we could be sisters.

"What kind of dog is that?" I ask.

"She's a silky terrier," says Gina.

"How old is she?"

"Five-and-a-half."

"Years?"

"Yes, years."

"Did you get her when she was a pup?"

Gina nods. "When she was just eight weeks old."

"And did you name her Lucy right away?"

"No, I called her George at first. It wasn't till after the sex change that I named her Lucy. Of course I called her

Lucy right away!" She's looking at me like I'm totally weird.

I guess I am sounding a bit strange. The thing that gets me, though, is that Lucy looks so much like me. I can't help feeling suspicious. It would be just like Gina to name her dog after me as some kind of a joke.

My mom grabs her jacket from the closet. She stoops down and pats the dog. "See, Lucy? Isn't she a darling little thing?"

This could get very confusing.

Gina is looking from her Lucy to me and back again. She starts to laugh. I give her my maddest look. It doesn't stop her.

"Look, Kate, your Lucy and my Lucy look like twins."

My mother sees my face and doesn't say anything.

I am totally insulted. Who wants to look just like a dog, even if she is kind of a cute dog?

"She had a poo about an hour ago," says Gina, "so she probably won't go again, but here are a couple of baggies, just in case."

She's got to be joking. There's no way I am picking up dog poop. And pooing is not what you'd call a polite topic of conversation. Does she think the whole world wants to know about her dog's bathroom habits? Then suddenly it hits me. Maybe I do need to know just a bit more.

"She won't go in the house, will she?"

"Oh no, she's a good girl," Gina says as she pushes the leash and plastic bags at me.

I take them to be polite. I won't be using them. There's no way I am taking this dog outside.

three

After Mom and Gina leave, the dog wanders around from room to room, sniffing everything. I follow her. I hope she's not looking for a place to go pee. If she goes in the house, I'm just going to leave the mess until my mom gets home. It was her idea to leave a dog here with me.

Maybe I'll phone Siobhan. She's my best friend, even if I mostly only see her at school. She has six younger brothers and sisters. There's always at least one of them who's still in diapers, so Siobhan is used to dealing with disgusting things. She'd know what to do if this dog does something on the floor.

I dial her number and two kids answer at once. Neither one will hang up. Neither one will call Siobhan. I hang up and after a few minutes I try again. This time Siobhan answers on the first ring.

"You wouldn't believe what my mom has dumped on me," I tell her.

"What?"

"I'm all alone here, looking after Gina's dog."

"Sounds like heaven." Something crashes in the background and a kid starts to cry. "Just hold on a minute," Siobhan says.

She's gone quite a long time. I watch the dog. Now she is sitting on the floor beside by my feet. She's watching me. When I look at her, her tail waves back and forth like one of those big feathers slaves used to fan rich people with. Her ears perk up like she's expecting me to say something interesting.

Siobhan is back. "Look, Lucy, I really can't talk right now."

"Could you come over?" I ask.

"No, I'm babysitting. My mom's out grocery shopping. Why don't you come over here? You could bring the dog."

"I don't have a ride. Dad won't be back till about eleven."

"Well, come over then, if you want." In the background, it sounds like the kids are fighting: one boy is yelling, someone else is bawling, one of the little girls is calling for Siobhan.

"Well, maybe not," I say. "You sound pretty busy."

"Oh, my mom will be back soon. If you can get here by noon, we can go down to the food court for lunch and then wander around the mall."

I don't really like going to the mall very much, but it's better than having to hang around her place with all those kids bugging us. And it's definitely better than sitting here looking at this stupid dog. "I'll ask Dad for a ride as soon as he gets back," I say.

The dog is still looking at me. I leave the kitchen and go up to my room. The dog follows me up the stairs, even though each step is a very big jump for her. I lie on my bed and turn on my TV. I'm flipping channels when I hear her make this funny grunting noise. I look over the edge of the bed at her. She's looking up at me with that look again: ears perked, head cocked to one side, her tail waving back and forth. She looks hard at me. I look back at her. She grunts again and does a little jump. I think she wants up on the bed. She can think again. That would be so unsanitary. Who knows what she's been walking in? Dogs get intestinal worms a lot too. Who knows what you might catch?

I find a show I want to watch and sit back against my pillows. The dog gives a bark. What now? I look down at her. She barks again. At first it's a bark every ten seconds or so. Then she gets more serious about it and just sits there looking at me, barking nonstop. Finally, I can't stand it anymore. I lean over and lift her up onto the bed. Right away, she turns in circles a few times and plops down. She's as nervy as Gina. At least she's quit barking and grunting. I settle down to watch my show. The dog looks up at me with her big brown eyes and then she shifts her body over so she's touching me. She gives a big sigh and closes her eyes to sleep. She's not so bad really.

My dad gets home about half an hour later. I run down to see if he'll give me a ride to Siobhan's. He parks the van and I rush outside to meet him, but before I can talk to him, a guy pulls up behind him in Mom's car. I'm expecting it to be one of the boys from the service station, not a strange man wearing a black shirt and a priest's collar. It's kind of a shock. I mean, I know priests don't get paid much, but I never thought their salaries were so bad they'd have to work at a garage to make extra money.

"I bumped into Father Tony down at the garage," Dad says. "He was waiting for his car anyway, so he offered to drive your mom's home for me."

By this time, the priest is out of the car and walking over to us.

"Father, this is my daughter, Lucy."

Suddenly, I'm feeling all shy, but still I say, "Pleased to meet you," even if I say it so quietly I'm not sure anyone hears me.

Father Tony doesn't seem to notice. He's looking at our house, telling Dad we have a nice place. We do. This is Greenwood Glade. It's a gated community. All the houses look perfect. If you don't maintain your home, I think you get kicked out.

I hear barking. I've left the dog alone inside. Will she chew things? I run to get her. I carry her back to the driveway because I'm not taking any chances with what she might do if I put her on the ground. She's not likely to poop while I'm holding her.

"Now who's this?" asks my dad.

"It's a dog. Gina's dog. We have to look after her because Mom and Gina are out hunting down packing boxes and there are a bunch of real estate agents touring her apartment."

"What time did your mom say she'd be back?"

"She didn't say."

Dad scratches the dog under her chin. "Cute little thing, isn't it?"

I'm just glad he hasn't said anything about her looking like me.

"I have to get Father Tony back to the service station," Dad says.

"Can you drive me to Siobhan's?" I ask. "And keep the dog till Mom gets home? She's no trouble really."

"Well, I think I can manage that." He turns to Father Tony. "It's on our way back to the garage anyway."

Dad holds the dog while I run in to get my bag and a jacket. When I come back, Dad and Father Tony are already belted into their seats. The dog is in the back.

"Father Tony has just come here from the seminary in Edmonton," Dad says. "He was at the garage this morning, getting his snow tires taken off."

Father Tony turns around in his seat so he can talk to me. "Father Mac tells me that you don't get snow-storms in April here."

"No," I say. "Not in April. Will you be staying at Saint Francis?"

If he's just come from the seminary, then he won't have had any practice being a priest, but Father Mac is ancient and it's good he's finally going to get to retire.

"Yes, I'm going to be the assistant pastor; it's a big parish and Father Mac can use some help. He tells me you haven't much by way of programs for teens in the parish. One of the things I hope to do this coming September is get a youth group started. You might be interested."

What does a youth group do? I'm not keen on signing up for more religion classes. "I go to Holy Name Secondary," I say. "I take religion there."

"I was thinking of more of a social group."

"Sounds interesting," I say. I am such a phoney! I'm not interested at all. I'm no good in crowds.

Dad pulls into Siobhan's driveway, and I go to get out.

"You have a great afternoon then, Lucy," says Father Tony. "And don't worry, I'm sure your dad will take good care of the little Lucy-dog here."

I feel like someone has dumped a bucket of ice water on me. "Why did you call her that?" I ask, trying to keep calm.

He laughs. "Well, you didn't tell us her name. And I couldn't help thinking she looks just like you would if you were to suddenly be turned into a dog."

"I see." That's all I say. I'm biting my tongue so hard I'm surprised it doesn't bleed. I turn my back on them and walk to Siobhan's door. Father Tony is not going to see *me* at his stupid youth group. He's not going to see me ever again, if I can help it.

Siobhan's mom is home. Siobhan can't wait to get out of the house, so we leave right away. It's about eight blocks to the mall. While we're walking, I tell Siobhan about how my mom is fighting with everyone. "I really think Gina's the cause of it all. She's a bad influence."

"You don't like her?" Siobhan asks.

"Not at all."

"Why not? What's wrong with her?"

"Well, she wears dresses that show most of her boobs and she goes to nightclubs and sits on her boyfriend's knee. Now she's moving in with him and they aren't even married."

Siobhan doesn't act as shocked as I thought she would.

"And she shows no respect for anything or anyone. You'll never guess what she named her dog."

"What?"

"Lucy!"

"You decided not to like her because of her dog's name?"

"Who'd name a dog Lucy?" I ask. "It just shows how ignorant she is."

Siobhan looks at me funny. "Mr. and Mrs. Murray on our street have a black lab named Lucy," she says. "My Uncle Max named his dog Lucy too." Siobhan's forehead is puckered up in a frown like she's thinking hard. Finally, she says, "Except for you, the only Lucys I know *are* dogs."

"What about the *I Love Lucy Show*?" I ask.

"When's that on?"

"Well, it's a really old show. I don't think it's on anymore. Grandma has it on VHS."

"So is the Lucy on that show a dog?"

I feel like hitting her.

"You could change your name," says Siobhan. "I'm going to change mine as soon as I'm old enough."

"What to?"

"I'm just going to change the spelling. Who knows how to say *S-i-o-b-h-a-n*? Anyone who sees my name in writing just calls me 'Hey You.' No one can spell it. Even half the teachers get it wrong. I'm going to change it so that it's spelled the way it sounds. *S-h-i-v-a-h-n*."

"That makes sense," I say.

"So would you like to change your name?"

Before I can answer, she stops in the middle of the sidewalk and shoves my shoulder so hard I take a fast step back onto the lawn of the house we're passing.

"Hey, I know another human named Lucy. Lucy Lawless. She's not a dog. She used to be the actress from *Xena: Warrior Princess*. Why don't you change your name to Xena? I don't know any dogs named Xena."

"I am not changing my name!" I'm gritting my teeth so tightly that it's a wonder I can pronounce the words. "People just ought to be more careful about what they call their dogs. Lucy was the name of a very famous saint. I was named after her."

Siobhan looks at me blankly. "Is that something I'm supposed to remember from religion class? Because if it is, I don't."

Siobhan sucks at religion. She's just not interested in it. I'm always a bit surprised by this. She's the one with six brothers and sisters. You'd think that would prove her family was really religious.

"I think they might have mentioned Saint Lucy back when we got to choose our confirmation names. I'm not sure," I say.

"So how do you know about her?"

"Grandma has all these books about saints. I read them when I'm at her house."

"This Saint Lucy, what did she do?"

"Well, she didn't do anything. I mean, that was the point. She was a virgin and martyr."

"What's the sense of that?"

"It proved she loved God. That's why she got to go straight to heaven."

A car slows down beside us. Siobhan looks over at the boys inside. She flips her hair and turns away in kind of a stuck up-way, except that she smiles when she does it. Siobhan's only six months older than I am, but she could pass easily for fifteen. She has everything I don't: boobs, hips, and long, wavy hair with lots of body.

"Hey, baby," one of the guys yells. Then they drive away.

I've just ignored them completely. I try to remember where I left off. "It's like this," I say. "Lucy loved God so much she wanted to devote her life to prayer instead of getting married and having a bunch of kids and having to cook and clean all the time."

"You can't blame her for that," says Siobhan.

"Nobody's blaming her for anything. She's a saint."

"I just meant, I could understand why she might not want to get married and have a gazillion kids."

I wish Siobhan wouldn't always interrupt me when I'm trying to explain things. "Anyway, her father was dead, and for some reason, she forgot to tell her mother that she planned to remain a virgin, so her mother went and arranged a marriage for her."

"I'd hate it if I had to marry someone my parents chose for me," Siobhan says.

"I think all the marriages in those days were arranged by the parents. But like I'm trying to tell you, when Lucy wouldn't marry the guy her mother picked, the guy told the king that she was a Christian and the king sent his soldiers to arrest her and take her away to be a prostitute."

"She became a prostitute and she still got to be a saint? That wouldn't happen these days. She'd probably start taking drugs and turn into a total mess."

"No, Lucy didn't become a prostitute. You see, when the soldiers came for her, they couldn't move her. She was too heavy."

"So she was really fat? That would be a major turn-off for most guys. She'd never get any customers."

"She wasn't fat!" I say. "She was just heavy."

She's missing the whole point of this story.

"Anyway, the king and his soldiers couldn't take Lucy away to be a prostitute, so they killed her instead. That's what makes her a martyr. She died because she wouldn't break her promise to God."

Siobhan's walking a little ahead of me. She stops so abruptly that I almost bump into her. She turns to face me. "Did she promise God she'd stay a virgin before or after her mother arranged the marriage?"

"Before, I think, but her mother didn't know about it."

"I bet she just didn't like the guy. Imagine if your parents were going to make you marry Rodney Blackstone."

"Oh, gross!" I say. Rodney's a guy from our school who's just a total pig. He's always picking his nose and eating the boogers. "Any girl would rather die than marry someone like him."

"So it wouldn't prove that you loved God at all."

I think about it. Grandma's book didn't say anything about what the guy looked like.

"What about that hot guy who's always riding his dirt bike up and down my street?" Siobhan asks. "Would you break your vow if it was him your mom was forcing you to marry?"

I know who she means. That guy is a total hunk. "Would you?" I ask.

"What vow?" says Siobhan. "I don't remember any vow."

She's got me giggling now.

Siobhan puts the palms of her hands together in front of her chest like she's praying. "Oh, dearest Mama, your wish is my command. If you absolutely insist that I marry that sexy beast, I will do my duty and obey."

We are laughing so loudly that some of the people driving by in cars are staring at us.

How did we get from talking about Saint Lucy to talking about sexy beasts? This was supposed to be a serious conversation. Grandma says everyone's goal in life should be to become a saint.

I try to think holy thoughts. It doesn't work. Without meaning to, I find myself thinking of other hot guys. It probably doesn't matter that much. I don't think I could be a saint anyway. I'd never be able to manage the part about being lit on fire and then stabbed a million times and left to die slowly in a prison cell. That's what happened to Saint Lucy in the end. About the time they lit the first match for the fire, I'd probably even be willing to reconsider Rodney Blackstone.

four

When we get back from the mall later in the afternoon, Siobhan's dad gives me a ride home. I notice right away that my mom's car is gone. When I get into the house, I see that the dog is gone too. Dad is sitting at the kitchen table just doing nothing.

"Where's Mom?" I ask.

"She's spending the night at Gina's."

This is just too much! "She was out with Gina last night. She spent almost all day with her today."

"Gina's not going to be at her apartment. She's at Ian's. Your mom says she needs some time alone."

"But what about us?" I look around the kitchen. It's after five o'clock, but there's no sign of dinner. "Did she leave something for us to heat up?"

"No," says Dad. He starts looking through the cupboards. "You must be hungry."

"I am."

"Do you feel like peanut butter sandwiches?" he asks.

"Do we have any bananas?"

"No."

Mom hasn't gone grocery shopping either.

He opens the fridge and we stand there together, looking into it.

"You must know how to cook something," I say. "You were single a long time before you married Mom. How did you look after yourself before?"

Suddenly he looks a bit happier, like I've given him an idea.

"You're right," he says. He grabs the phone book and finds the restaurant section. Then he slides it across the counter so I can see it too. Some of the ads include menus.

"See anything you'd like?" he asks.

"How about Italian?" I say.

We choose a restaurant that is not too far away and delivers. We look over their ad and decide on ribs, spaghetti, and Caesar salad. He phones in the order.

While we wait, Dad sits down at the computer and I watch TV.

Twenty minutes later, the doorbell rings. Dinner is served.

We help ourselves from the takeout cartons. The food's not bad. I finish all of mine, but Dad hardly eats at all.

"It's not as good as homemade, is it?" I ask. "Don't you like it?"

He acts a bit startled. We haven't been talking, and it's as if he's been daydreaming. "Oh, no," he says. "It's fine. I'm just not very hungry."

He scrapes all the leftover food from his plate into the garbage, and I load the dishwasher. He wanders to the window and looks into the backyard. Then he picks up the newspaper that's still on the table from this morning. He gets the scissors and a pen from the kitchen drawer and clips out *The New York Times* crossword. He puts the scissors back and sits down to do the puzzle. He fills in a few spaces. Then he leaves everything on the table and goes to the living room and picks up a book he's been reading. He spends maybe five minutes with the book and then puts that down too. He picks up the remote control and starts channel surfing. There's not much on TV except news.

"Why don't we go over to Grandma and Granddad's?" I suggest. I'm thinking that Grandma would at least play cards with me.

"I don't think that would be a good idea," Dad says.

"Why not?"

"They'll want to know where your mom is, and I don't feel like explaining."

I'd do the explaining, I think to myself. I don't have a problem with that. I'm very close to my grandmother. When I was born, Grandma quit her job to stay home and look after me while Mom finished school. We lived with Grandma and Granddad until I was six. I still stay with her after school every day until my mom and dad get home from work.

My dad likes Grandma too. I think she sort of arranged for him to marry Mom. When I was five, my granddad was the financial chairman of the parish council. It was up to him to arrange the annual audit of the parish's books. He contacted the bank, and they referred him to an accountant named Harold Jensen. Harold was twenty-six, he was single, and he was Catholic. As Grandma says, "The Lord provides."

Granddad brought Harold home for dinner. Mom says that Granddad did the dishes for the first time in his life that night. Grandma forgot her rules about me being Mom's responsibility and insisted on putting me to bed. She wouldn't even let Mom help, and Mom was left to entertain Harold. She was furious. (My mother is often furious. Grandma says she's a true O'Connor. Mom's got Granddad's Irish temper.) Mom says she felt like she was being offered on a platter. When she says this, Dad replies that she was the best part of dinner. He must have talked her out of her bad mood because the rest is history. I was the flower girl at their wedding. I love looking at the pictures from that day. I had this poufed white dress and a little veil held in place by a comb with pink satin roses attached to it. I looked just darling.

I sit down with Dad and we stare at the TV screen. A hockey game is on. Neither of us is in to sports, but we're just too lazy to change the channel.

"What would you think of going to mass this evening?" he asks.

"Why would we do that?"

"I wouldn't mind hearing Father Tony. You might like it. He says the music at the Saturday night service is pretty lively. A lot of the young people go to that mass."

"Did you hear what he said to me when I got out of the car? About the Lucy-dog?"

"Yeah, he thought it was funny that Gina's dog looks so much like you. What's her name?"

"I just call her Dog."

"Well, want to go to mass?"

"I guess," I answer. It's not like I'll have to speak to Father Tony, and I suppose it will be at least as interesting as sitting here, watching Dad fidget. It will give me a chance to pray for my mom too. She needs it.

It feels funny going to church at the wrong time on the wrong day, but once we're inside, it's about the same. I ask for fifty cents from my dad and light some candles in the rack in front of the statue of Our Lady. Then I pray. I ask Jesus to speak to Mom's heart and remind her to look to Mary, who is the model of what every woman should be. You wouldn't see Mary running off to pilates classes or leaving Jesus and Joseph just because she wanted time to herself.

Praying makes me feel much better. When I get back to the pew where my dad is sitting, the choir is setting up. It's nothing like the one on Sunday morning, where old ladies sing along to a very slow and tired-sounding organ. Tonight there are guitars, a flute, and drums, and most of the singers and players are in their teens. It's a much livelier performance. When mass is over, Father Tony stands in the vestibule, shaking hands with people. Dad goes up and says something to him, but I pretend I'm reading the notices on the bulletin board and then sneak past while Father Tony's talking to someone else.

If you go to mass Saturday night, you don't have to go Sunday. It would be the same Bible readings and the same talk anyway. I sleep in late the next morning because no one comes to wake me up and because the house is so quiet. It's way too quiet. I call Grandma as soon as I get up, and she says she'll pick me up for lunch. I stay at her place all afternoon. We drink about a million pots of tea and talk about Mom. Grandma's as confused as I am about all of this. I mean, maybe Mom didn't have much fun as a teenager, but she has a good life now. We have a beautiful house in sort of a snobby neighborhood. She has the perfect job, working with all those nice old nuns at the convent. We're all healthy. True, she and Dad haven't been able to have babies, but like Grandma says, they're lucky enough to have me, even if I did come along early. What more could she want?

"A life!" Mom replies when I ask her later.

She's home alone when Granddad drops me off. I find her up in her room. She's folding clothes.

"But you can't go backward," I say. "You can't be sixteen again."

"What are you talking about?"

"Well, Grandma says you're probably feeling like you never had a childhood. You know, like you missed out on being a normal teenager."

"That's what the two of you figured out, is it? I suppose you spent all afternoon talking about how to deal with me, like I'm some sort of problem child."

That's kind of true.

"I'm not worried about what I missed when I was sixteen. I'm miserable about what I'm missing now. I feel like I've been buried alive."

"You're depressed."

She stops what she's doing for a second and looks at me. "Then you do understand."

"Sure, it's probably just some kind of a chemical imbalance. There are pills for that."

Mom glares at me. Her lips disappear completely. This is not a good sign, but she doesn't say anything.

"Depression's pretty common. Lana from my math class takes an antidepressant. She says she feels much better."

Mom spins around and walks over to her closet. She pulls down a suitcase. "Pills," she mutters. "She wants me to take pills."

"What are you doing?" I ask. That's a stupid question, I realize. I can see exactly what she's doing. She's putting folded clothes into the suitcase. "Where are you going?"

She sits down on her bed and looks at me. "I don't know how to explain this to you . . . how to help you understand . . ."

"I understand just fine. You want to divorce Dad and start going to nightclubs like Gina does. You don't care about me and Dad at all."

"Of course I care about you!"

She reaches out to put her arms around me, but I twist away and run into my room. I throw myself down face-first on my bed. I'm crying, but it's mostly because I'm mad. She doesn't follow me. When I calm down, I sit up and take a good look around.

I happen to have the coolest bedroom in the world. Mom and Dad worked on it for weeks. It's all totally color coordinated in apple green and sky blue. Mom got decorator baskets for my odds and ends, and Dad cut out round pieces of corkboard for the wall above my desk. They are painted in the exact shades of the pattern on my bedspread and curtains. I have lots of cushions and a funky lamp Mom made. Dad built all the shelves and the study nook.

I suppose she expects me to leave all this behind and sleep on a couch or something. Gina's apartment is really tiny.

Mom comes into my room. She doesn't say anything; she just puts an empty suitcase on my bed, opens it, and starts toward my closet.

"What do you think you're doing?" I ask.

"I'm getting you enough clothes to last the week."

"Don't bother. I'm not going anywhere."

She stops and just stands there in front of the closet with her back to me. Finally, she turns around. "Who'll drive you to school?" she asks. "Who'll make your breakfast and pack your lunch?"

"Well, if you cared, you'd stay and there wouldn't be a problem."

"I'm not staying, Lucy, so we better pack up some things for you."

"I'm not going anywhere. We'll manage somehow. I'm sure Grandma will help out."

Her shoulders sag. She closes the empty suitcase and takes it back to her room.

I don't follow her. I lie face-down on my bed and act like I'm crying. I'm thinking maybe this will make her change her mind. I'm wrong.

I hear a door close downstairs. I run down to check, and by the time I get to the kitchen, I hear her car start up. I go through to the living room and watch her drive away. Then I go upstairs, throw myself across the bed, and start really crying.

It's six o'clock before my dad comes home. He's surprised to see me.

"I thought your mom was taking you with her," he says.

"She was going to, but I didn't want to go."

He puts a very small bag of groceries down on the kitchen island. "I was just going to make hot dogs for dinner."

"Hot dogs will be fine."

While Dad gets them ready, I imagine Mom eating all alone. She's probably already starting to feel sorry she left. "I bet she won't last more than a day or two," I say.

I think Dad knows what I'm talking about, but he doesn't answer. He's busy grabbing the pan of hot dog buns from out of the oven. There's a lot of smoke, and the buns are all burned on top. He tosses them in the garbage and gets four more out of the pack on the counter. He turns the temperature down and tries again.

Mom calls the next night at about eight.

"Did you and your dad go out for dinner tonight?" she asks.

"No, I ate at Grandma's. Dad's making himself a sandwich."

"I called an hour ago and there was no answer. When did you get home?"

"About ten minutes ago. *Some* people take their responsibilities seriously, you know. Dad had to work late."

Dad works horrible hours every April because that's when he has to do income tax returns for all his clients. It is his busiest time of year.

"I hope Grandma and Granddad don't mind you staying so late. Did they say anything about it?"

"No, why would they? Grandma probably appreciated the company. Granddad was in a rotten mood and just went back down to his den in the basement as soon as he finished dinner. If I hadn't been there, Grandma would have been sitting by herself all evening."

My mother gets her bad temper from Granddad O'Connor. He doesn't yell as much as she does, but that's probably because he's more mature. Even so, you can tell right away if he is mad about something. A lot of people would call him a grouch, but Grandma says we should always try to see the image of Jesus in people. With Granddad, it's not easy. Mostly when he is grumpy, I just ignore him.

"Dad's eating a ham and cheese sandwich," I tell Mom. "That's what he packed for his lunch too. He doesn't even put lettuce in them. He hasn't eaten a single vegetable all day."

"Well, check the crisper and see if there are some baby carrots left. If you can't find any of those, get him a couple of pickles. You take care. I'll call you tomorrow."

And she does call. She calls at the same time every evening, but she never says she's sorry she left or that she's going to come home.

At school, my friend Mariah tells Siobhan and me that Mom's supposed to have access visits. Mariah's parents have been separated for years. She lives with her mom, but she has to visit her dad every second weekend. She says that's always how it's done.

Thursday night, I ask my dad if he and Mom have discussed access.

"You can see your mom whenever you want," he says.

"I don't think that's how you're supposed to do it. You two should have a schedule. Like if I live with you, Mom should get to have me weekends."

"If you want to see your mom for the weekend, why don't you call her?"

"I think we need to go to court about it. Mariah, a girl in my class whose parents are divorced, says her parents have a court order that sets out all the days she has to visit her dad."

Dad doesn't answer me. He just goes to find our phone book and starts flipping through it. Then he punches in a number and waits.

"Kate?" There's a little pause. "Lucy has been check- ing out the rules for separated parents. We're not doing it right." He gives a little laugh.

It's the first time all week I've seen him even smile.

"No," he says, "for once I don't think it was Grandma she consulted. It seems a girl in her class is the resident expert on the subject. She's told Lucy I should be giving you access visits. Want to talk to Lucy?"

He hands me the phone.

"Would you like to come over after school tomor- row and stay the weekend?" Mom asks.

"Would you pick me up from Grandma's?"

"You were with me once when I stopped by Gina's," she says. "Remember where it is? It's only two blocks from your school. You can walk. I'll call Grandma and tell her she doesn't have to pick you up."

"But won't you still be at work?"

"Just ring the manager. I'll leave my key so she can let you in. Lucy will be so glad to see you. It's a long day for her all by herself."

"Lucy?"

"The dog."

"I thought you said Gina was moving in with her boyfriend."

"She did, but Ian's building doesn't allow pets. They're looking for something bigger anyway, but in the meantime, I said I'd look after Lucy."

So Mom's abandoned Dad and me, but she doesn't mind looking after Gina's dog. I bet that dog's been eating better than Dad has. And I suppose she makes a fuss over her and takes her for walks. The dog's probably had way more attention than I've had this past week. I'm about to tell her what I think about her caring more for a dog than for her own daughter, but she asks what I'd like for dinner tomorrow. I cave, and I ask for vegetarian lasagna. She says she'll make a salad to go with it. She is very big on vegetables. This meal will make up for the last few days of Dad's cooking. I don't want to get that disease where your teeth fall out because you've had no vitamin C.

five

Once I start down the street toward Gina's apartment the next day, I realize I didn't need to write down her address when I was on the phone with Mom. It's the only apartment building on the block. When I get to the door, I ring the manager's suite, and when a lady says hello through the intercom, I tell her who I am. She tells me to come to suite 101 and she buzzes me in.

As I approach her suite, I can see her standing in her hallway through her open front door. I'm glad I get to see her from a distance first. If I'd had to knock on her door for her to answer, I'd have been there with my nose at the height of her belt buckle. She's that tall. Big boned too. I look up at her and give a polite smile.

She is grinning at me like it's all she can do to keep from laughing. "Well, I guess I can hand the key over without demanding any ID from you. Aren't you the image of your mother?"

I am not the image of my mother. I have stick-straight, blondish, reddish, brownish hair. My mom has curly auburn hair. Grandma says it would be tidier if she wore it short, but Dad likes it the way it is, kind of wild and longish. "I don't think we look that much alike," I say.

"Well, look at the size of you," the manager says.

I feel like saying, "And look at the size of *you!*" but she'd probably tell my mom and then I'd get in trouble. My mother is five-feet tall. I'm still hoping I'll catch up with her someday. We're both kind of skinny too, except Mom has nice boobs. I'm also hoping I'll catch up with her there.

"Maybe you can convince Gina to give you that dog for good," the manager says. "She'd be a fit."

"Thank you," I say, holding out my hand. She's still holding on to the key. I'm lucky. She takes the hint and hands it to me. I head for the elevator.

I have a little trouble with the lock, and that stupid dog standing on the other side of the door, barking her head off, doesn't help. I'm such a wreck worrying about the noise that it's not until I get the door open and the dog is jumping all over my legs that I realize she might have turned vicious having a stranger come into her apartment. But she doesn't bite me. Mostly she's just way too excited. She runs across the room to this little basket of dog toys and brings one of them to me. She drops it at my feet and then lowering her chest on the floor, keeping her bum in the air, she starts barking again. I pick up the toy. It's a yellow chicken, the kind kids get in their Easter baskets. The dog is going crazy, barking and running around me in circles. I throw the chicken. The whole apartment's not much bigger than my mom's bedroom at home, so it only takes the dog about two seconds to get the chicken and bring it back to me. She barks. I'm supposed to throw it again. We do this about ten times. If I don't throw the chicken fast enough, she barks at me. How long am I supposed to keep this up? My mom's not going to be home for another half hour.

I decide to try and ignore her. I find a note from my mom on the table. It says if the dog is driving me crazy, I can take her for a walk, that it will calm her down. The chicken's at my feet and the dog's barking again. She could definitely drive me crazy. Mom's left the leash on the table by the note. I pick it up. The dog sees it and forgets all about her chicken. She runs to the door. She stands there, and when I don't follow her right away, she starts barking again. I can see why Ian's apartment doesn't allow dogs. I wouldn't be surprised if the real reason Gina's moved is because she's been kicked out of this place.

I snap the leash onto the dog's collar. Mom's left two plastic bags on the table and I know why they're there. I leave them. If we just walk for a few minutes, maybe the dog won't do anything. If she does, I'll just pretend not to notice. I can't be watching her every second, can I?

I don't know why they say that having a dog is good exercise. Mostly this one just runs around in circles. She sniffs here, she pees there, then she goes back and has another sniff – and all this time I've walked maybe five steps. At least she isn't barking. Gina's apartment building takes up most of the block. Next to it, there's one of those monster houses that people are always complaining about. It's white stucco with an orange tiled roof. There are also a few old-fashioned bungalows, but most of the houses on this block are big ones like this. We're halfway past it when the dog stops to sniff a spot on the lawn. She spreads her feet, lowers her bum down, and raises her tail. She's going to go.

I pretend to look at the traffic. The "traffic" is just one green SUV. I watch it drive all the way down the block. I sneak a peek at the dog. She's still going. Does she have to take forever? I admire the blossoms on a flowering cherry tree in the yard next door. Finally, she's done. Now we just have to get out of here.

We aren't fast enough. We only get about ten feet when this old woman in a silver-gray sari comes out the front door of the house. She's talking in some foreign language so I don't know what she's saying, but it's pretty clear that she's mad at me. She's pointing back to the place where the dog pooped and then at the house.

Two younger women come out. One of them is carrying a little kid. The three women are yelling at me but not in English, and they come right up to me. The dog's barking, but she's not much protection. I'm scared. I don't know what to do.

"I'm sorry," I say. "I don't understand."

They all keep talking. Some people from the house next door have come out onto their balcony to watch. Across the street, other neighbors are pulling their curtains back to see what's happening.

I just stand there with these three women crowded around me. I can hardly breathe. I want to walk away, but they're blocking my way. The dog's quit barking. Even though this is all her fault, she's wandering from one person to the next, wagging her tail and trying to look innocent. The women must realize I don't understand because they start talking more to each other than to me. Finally, a boy who's just a bit older than me comes out of the house. He says something to the women. One of them answers him, and then they all go quiet.

He turns to me. "They're angry because you didn't pick up after your dog."

"She's not mine," I tell him.

"Well, you're walking her. You brought her here to poop on our lawn. You're responsible."

I can feel my cheeks heating up. "I didn't bring her to poop on your lawn. She decided to do that on her own."

The woman with the little kid on her hip starts talking again. She points to the child and then to the dog.

"She says that there are small children living here," says the boy. "With people like you around, she says, we can't let the kids play in their own yards. They'll get covered in dog poop."

I look at the dog. "She's a very small dog," I say. "It's not like she's left poop all over the yard."

"Since it's such a little bit, you shouldn't mind picking it up."

That isn't what I meant at all. "I forgot to bring a bag."

The boy yells to a couple of younger kids who have been watching us from the front door of the house. A few seconds later, one of them comes out, walks toward us, and hands the boy a plastic bag.

I give my bravest smile. "Thank you so much."

I think he's going to clean it up for me. I'm wrong. He hands me the bag.

I go back to the dog's little pile of poop. How am I supposed to get it in the bag? I look around the yard and sidewalk.

"What are you looking for?" the boy asks.

"A stick or something to scoop it in with."

He throws his arms out and says something in the foreign language to the women. They all laugh. He takes the bag from me and puts his hand in it. He shows me how you're supposed to pick the stuff up and then turn the bag inside out so the poop is inside. It would have been better if he'd demonstrated on the real thing, but no. Instead, he just does it in the air and gives the bag back to me. Everyone is watching: not just all the people in this family but a lot of the neighbors too. I pick up the poop the way he showed me, and I knot the bag. Everyone cheers.

"Bravo!" the boy says. He's laughing. "Now that wasn't so bad, was it?"

I disagree, but I guess he's trying to be nice, so I just shrug.

"My name's Rob," he says.

The old woman shakes her finger at him. "Ravindra," she says. She looks at me but points at him, "Ravindra."

"Okay, okay," he says. "My real name is Ravindra, but my friends call me Rob."

"What do your enemies call you?" I ask.

He just laughs. "You're not going to hold a grudge, are you? What's your name?"

The rest of the family is going back to the house, so there's just the two of us now. "Lucy."

He looks at the bag of dog doo-doo in my hand. "I think I'll pass on shaking hands." Then he starts to laugh again.

I see my mom's car coming down the street. She waves and stops in front of us. We'll only be driving the half-block back to the apartment entrance, but I pick up the dog and climb in. I hand her the bag of poop.

Rob waves good-bye.

"It's so easy to meet new people when you have a dog," Mom says.

She doesn't know the half of it.

SIX

We actually have a pretty good evening. At dinnertime, I eat so much that Mom says I really must have missed her. She's rented a chick flick and she makes popcorn. It's way better than watching Dad working on people's tax returns.

After the movie, I'm feeling ready for bed. "Where are we sleeping?" I ask.

There's only one bed and it's in a bit of an alcove, not a proper bedroom.

"You can have the bed," Mom says. "I'll take the couch."

"I can't believe you actually expected me to move in here with you. It's so tiny!"

"Yeah, it's beginning to get to me," says Mom. "There's no room for anything, and of course I have to keep the place super neat because I never know when the realtor will be showing it. I've been looking for something more permanent."

"Permanent? Like you're never coming home?"

I don't do it on purpose, but I just can't help myself and I start bawling. After such a nice evening, I'd been sure she'd be thinking it was time for her to come back to Dad and me. Mom puts her arm around my shoulder, but as soon as I get my tears under control, I push her away and try to talk some sense into her.

"You're supposed to work at a marriage. That's what Grandma . . ."

I stop. I remember what Dad said about it bugging Mom when I tell her what Grandma says. I try again.

"I'm sure now that Dad knows how important it is to you, he'd give you a special allowance so you can go to Starbucks after all your pilates classes. And if he knows you're going out for coffee with Gina, he'll probably be fine with you not getting home till nine."

"Oh, Lucy, it's not about going to Starbucks. You don't think I'd break up your home for something as silly as that, do you?"

That's exactly what I think. "Maybe you could talk to Father Mac about it, get some marriage counseling," I say.

Mom makes a rude face. "As if he'd understand any of it. I've already got your dad and grandma running my life. I'm not looking for someone else to tell me what to do."

We'd probably keep arguing, except just then the phone rings. Mom gets it. It's almost ten o'clock. Nobody ever calls us that late. I'm wondering who it is, but I don't wonder long because the second thing Mom says is, "Oh, hi, Dad. This is a surprise."

Granddad never phones.

I nudge Mom and mouth, "Is something wrong with Grandma?" I'm worried she's hurt herself or had a heart attack or something.

Mom shakes her head. "No." She's not saying anything, just listening. I'm listening too. Granddad's so loud I can hear a lot of what he's saying, and I wish I couldn't.

It's something about him having had enough of Mom's bloody nonsense and about him being tired of seeing Grandma always having to pick up the slack for her.

I can tell that Mom is getting mad, but she's having a hard time getting a word in. Yelling won't help her. Granddad is just naturally loud, and he never stops to listen. If Mom tries to talk, even if she yells, he'll raise his voice and talk over her. Instead, she tries to fit in a word here and there when he's taking a breath.

"I didn't know . . . I see your point. No . . . no. Okay. Well, I'm sorry . . . I'll look into it."

She doesn't say good-bye. I don't know if she's hung up on Granddad or Granddad has hung up on her.

She stands there for a minute, taking deep breaths. I bet she's counting to ten. There are tears in her eyes. She wipes away one that is about to run down her cheek, gives a sniff, and goes over to the sink to get herself a glass of water.

"That was Granddad," she says.

"I know. What was he on about?" I say this like I

don't already know. Like he said, he's mad at Mom because she's left Dad and Grandma is having to pick up the slack for her. I'm not stupid. Grandma is not cleaning our house or doing our laundry or grocery shopping. The only thing that's been different for her this last week is that I've been there longer than usual each day. I'm "the slack" she's been picking up. He makes it sound like I'm a piece of garbage.

"He says you've been there with Grandma till seven-thirty or eight o'clock every night this week," Mom says.

I nod. "Well, you know what it's like. Dad doesn't get home from work till six-thirty even on his good days, and this week he's had to put in some overtime hours." What I don't say is that it might get worse. It's tax time. All accountants work crazy hours in April. Mom knows this as well as I do.

"Granddad says it's too much for Grandma. She went to the doctor this afternoon and her blood pressure is way too high."

"Well, I'm not the one who made it high."

It's not like I'm a little kid and Grandma has to look after me. We just visit. She'd be making dinner anyway. An extra pork chop in the pan and another potato in the pot isn't any more work. I help load the dishwasher after we eat.

"If Grandma's blood pressure is high, it's because she's worried sick about you and Dad. And Granddad doesn't help. How does he think she feels when he's so crabby all the time?"

Mom ignores what I say about her upsetting Grandma. "Well, Granddad says he's worried about her being tired out, but you might have a point. I think partly he's mad because Grandma spends so much time with you that she's never free to go places or do things with him."

"She can go places with him. Where does he want to go? I could probably go with them . . ."

Mom rolls her eyes. I hate it when she does that. "We have to think of some different arrangements for next week."

I can't really argue with that. I don't believe for a minute that Grandma doesn't want me at her house so much. Still, if Granddad's going to get all twisted out of shape just because I don't get picked up at my usual time, he'll upset Grandma and her blood pressure will get even worse.

It's almost midnight, but now I can't get to sleep, even though I was really tired before Granddad called. My mind is just going at warp speed. What Granddad said about me just keeps going around and around in my head. He really hurt my feelings. I'm trying to think of something mean I could say to him, to let him know how it feels to be insulted and made to feel like garbage.

Gina's bed is way lower than my bed at home. The stupid dog can jump up onto it, and she does. She plops down close to me. If she thinks she's sleeping here, she can think again. I push her onto the floor.

Granddad's words are still in my ears. I remember now what he said first about being tired of Mom's nonsense.

That is one part he got right. I'm tired of her nonsense too. And he's got a point: she's the one who should be home making my dinner and keeping me company. Suddenly I'm feeling better about the whole thing. I'm glad he gave Mom an earful. It will give her something to think about. She hasn't listened to me, but maybe Granddad will have more influence.

The dog jumps up on my bed again. I go to push her off with my foot. Who wants her?

Sometimes when I'm having a mean thought, I think God just sort of rewinds a scene in my head and plays it back for me so I hear the words I've been thinking — as if they were said out loud by another person. It's like that now.

"Who wants her?" What an awful thing to think about a poor dog. I'm going to start crying again. The dog is just like me. Gina's walked off and left her behind. Now I'm shoving her off the bed and thinking mean thoughts about her.

I don't give her a push after all. I just turn over on my side and wait to see what she'll do. She curls up in a ball, right in the crook of my knees. I suppose I'll have to stay in this position all night. What if I roll over in my sleep? Will she have enough sense to move so I don't squash her? I guess she does, because when I wake up next morning, she's curled up against my stomach.

*

Sunday morning, Mom says she'll make Belgian waffles if I walk the dog. If I knew how to make waffles, I'd tell her to walk the dog herself. But I don't, so instead, I get the privilege of taking the dog for her first walk of the day. She hasn't been out since nine-thirty last night. What are the chances she'll hold off on the pooping for a couple of hours until the next time Mom walks her? Not good. I take one of the plastic bags that Mom has left by the leash on the table.

"There's a dumpster by the side entrance," Mom says. "Throw the poopy bag in that when you get back."

I wonder how long it will be before I start talking about dog doo-doo and "poopy bags." I'd like to think it couldn't happen to me. Gina better claim her dog soon. Still, since the dog goes and I do clean up after her, I think I deserve some credit for dealing with it, so I tell Mom later while we're eating our waffles. I can't believe I can talk about poop and eat at the same time.

Later in the day, Mom calls Dad and they arrange to meet after mass tomorrow morning and go for coffee. I'm so happy that I don't even get upset when, a few minutes later, she calls Grandma to ask if I can go stay with her and Granddad. Mom says she and Dad need to talk in private. I just hope Granddad will be able to manage having to "pick up the slack" one more time if it means maybe Mom and Dad might work things out.

After mass the next day, I stay at Grandma and

Granddad's until almost five o'clock. When Dad comes to pick me up, I'm kind of disappointed. As soon as we're alone, I tell him that.

"I feel kind of let down," I say. "I was hoping you and Mom would be together when you picked me up."

"Hmm?"

"Well, you see, Friday night Granddad gave Mom a real talking to. He said he and Grandma were tired of her nonsense, so I thought that's why she wanted to talk to you. She said you needed to work things out."

"She just meant we needed to work out our schedule with you."

I digest this information for awhile, but later, after we get home, I get thinking about it some more.

"If Mom just wanted to talk about my schedule, why couldn't I be there?" I ask. "That makes no sense."

"We talked about selling the house too."

My heart stops beating for a full minute. I sit down; otherwise I'll probably fall down. They can't sell this house; it's my home!

"It's not something we want to do, but we don't have any choice. We can't afford to keep it. We could manage the mortgage payments with both our salaries and if we counted our pennies, but it was always pretty tight. Now your mom will need her money to pay rent on her new place. I can't keep up the payments here on my own."

"What if Mom moved here instead? I could stay here with her and maybe you could get a small apartment."

Dad shakes his head. "There just isn't enough money to go around. We can't afford this place if either of us has to pay rent somewhere else."

"But what if Mom changes her mind and wants to come home?"

"I'm not holding my breath on that one," Dad replies. "She says she's got plans. They don't seem to include me. She's going to call a realtor tomorrow."

And just like that, Dad walks out of the room and leaves me sitting there by myself. I can imagine how bad he's feeling, so I don't take it as an insult or anything. He and Mom both worked so hard fixing up this place. No wonder he's upset. First he loses his wife; now he's losing his home. What I don't get is how Mom can walk away from it like it's no big deal. She loved this house so much, but I guess if you can fall out of love with your husband, you can fall out of love with your house too.

So in a day or two, we'll have a realtor tromping through our house. The realtor will love my room, I know it. I can hear his spiel now.

"This is an exceptional bedroom that was designed with a teenage girl in mind. Notice the study nook and all the custom-made shelving."

I imagine some other girl my age living here . . . in my room. I feel tears coming. I hate her. I hate the realtor. I hate my mother.

seven

It's Wednesday morning and I can't find my homework. I did it yesterday afternoon at Grandma's place. Maybe I left it there. When Dad drops me off at Grandma's again, she and I search for it, with no luck. Maybe it is at my mom's. I'm ready to scream! I am a very organized person, but there are limits. It's impossible to keep track of all my belongings living like this. Mom and Dad worked out my schedule. Dad takes me to Grandma's in the morning like always, then she takes me to school and picks me up again after school. Mom comes to get me from Grandma's place about five o'clock, when she gets off work. We go to her apartment and she feeds me dinner. When Dad gets off work, which could be any time between seven and nine o'clock, he picks me up from Mom's and takes me home to sleep.

"It's called joint custody," Mariah tells me one day over lunch at school.

"Well, I call it insanity! See this sandwich?" I ask. I wave it in front of them. "My mom made it. She's living two blocks from here, but this sandwich has traveled thirty-five miles to get here today. I had to take it home to Dad's. Then this morning, I had to remember to take it to Grandma's, and I was so busy trying to find my homework, I almost left it there."

"Think of the plus side," says Siobhan.

"And what would that be?"

"It's the perfect excuse for not having your homework, wouldn't you say? Sister Alexis didn't even give you a hard time about it."

Sometimes I wonder why Siobhan and I are friends. She can be so irresponsible.

"I probably shouldn't even care about them selling our house," I say. "I can just live in a car somewhere. That's pretty much what I'm doing now."

"If the place your mom is staying in is only two blocks from here, why is your grandma still picking you up from school every day?" Mariah asks. "Wouldn't it be simpler just to walk to your mom's?"

Well, obviously! That's what I did when I visited Mom last Friday. "You're right," I say. "I don't know why we're doing it this way. It makes no sense at all. Maybe we're all just so stressed out we're losing our minds."

"Maybe you're all stressed out, but at least your parents don't seem to fight that much. My dad and mom are back in court next week."

"What's it about this time?" Siobhan asks.

"The August long weekend."

"Why's that a problem?"

"Dad has me for July and Mom has me for August. Dad wants to bring me back after the long weekend. Mom says I have to be home by seven o'clock at night on July 31 because she gets me for August and he's not entitled to take extra days any time he wants."

"So what day is July 31?" Siobhan asks.

"Sunday."

I try to imagine both my parents wanting to be with me so much that they'd go to court to get an extra day or two of my company. It just wouldn't happen.

"At least you know they both want you. I feel like I'm some sort of a burden."

"Oh, come on, Lucy," says Siobhan. "You're not saying you feel like your parents don't want you, are you?"

"Well, not really, I guess . . ."

Siobhan reaches over and pats my hand. She leaves her hand on top of mine and gives it a squeeze. "It will be easier once your mom finds a bigger place and you can move in with her."

She's right of course. When Mom first left, I made a big deal about staying with Dad, but it really makes no sense at all. I only did that because I thought it would make Mom stay. So much for that plan. We haven't discussed it, but it's like everyone in my family knows that I'm going to be going with Mom as soon as she finds a place.

*

That night, when Mom picks me up from Grandma's, instead of going back to the apartment, we go to the house. For a crazy moment, I think maybe she's changed her mind and we're both going home. I'm wrong.

"Gina's realtor specializes in selling condo units, but he gave me a number for a woman in his firm who he says will do a good job marketing the house for us. She's coming by this evening."

"When Dad gets home?"

"Right."

"What's she like?" I'm getting ready to hate her, just like I planned.

"I don't know. I haven't talked to her. I gave your dad her number, so he's the one who set up the appointment."

"Why are we going there now? What about dinner?"

"It's in the back seat."

I look behind me. There's a submarine sandwich bag.

"I want to do a fast cleanup before she goes through the place."

"You mean, you're just coming over to do housework?"

"Well, I'll have to be there to sign the listing agreement anyway. She'll probably suggest a better price if things look good."

And maybe if things look messy enough, I think to myself, *no one will buy the house and I can stay there.* It's a stupid idea. If no one buys it and Dad can't make the payments, the bank will take it over and I'll still have to move.

"I'm going to come by and clean every weekend till the house sells," Mom says, "But until then, it's important that you and your dad keep it really tidy. You'll never know when they might be bringing people through."

"It would be easier if you'd move into a place big enough for both of us. If I'm not here, Dad will probably spend all his time at the office. The house will never get messy, and that way the realtor can bring people by without disturbing anyone."

"Good point. Dad's not the one who leaves a trail of clothing and books from the front door to the kitchen and then up to his bedroom when he gets home each day."

It bugs her when I do that. I can't help it if I have too much stuff to carry. When I put my backpack down on the hall table or hang my jacket over the railing of the stairway, I mean to come back for them – but then I get busy doing something else. It's easy to forget.

After we eat our sandwiches, Mom starts hauling out the vacuum. It makes me wonder what will happen when she gets her own place. Will she and Dad divide up all the furniture and the pots and pans and towels?

"When you find a place to rent and we move, who'll get the vacuum?"

Mom looks down at the old canister vacuum at her feet. "Me, I guess. I'm the only one in the family who knows how to turn it on."

She thinks she's being funny. The on/off switch is totally obvious.

"I don't mean just the vacuum. I mean every-thing. Will we take half the furniture and the dishes and all that?"

"I'm not going to take much right now," she answers. "The house looks better furnished."

I think about it. "If we took my bedspread and the baskets and cushions from my room, it wouldn't look so cool. It's the way it's all coordinated that makes it special."

"Right, and it's the same with the towels and bath mats in the bathrooms."

It's the same in every room. My mom has decorated the place to the max.

She hands me a dust cloth. "Here," she says. "Follow me around. You can dust while I vacuum."

I'm not amused. We start on the living room. I run the dust cloth over the top of the coffee table, weaving in and around the stuff she has on it.

"Lucy! Pick up that vase and the candles. Dust under them and then dust everything before you set it all back down again."

That's the trouble with all Mom's special touches. It would be much easier to dust at Siobhan's house. They don't have any ornaments. The kids have broken them all.

Mom finishes vacuuming the living room and front hall. She goes in and starts scrubbing the downstairs bathroom. I start dusting the end table between the wing chairs.

It's after six when Dad comes home. He's brought Chinese food. He offers Mom and me some, but we tell him we've already had dinner. He fills a plate for himself and stands over the kitchen sink, eating. He's just finished putting his plate in the dishwasher when the doorbell rings. He goes to answer it. Mom gives the counters one last wipe.

The woman at the door is tall and slim. She could be a fashion model, she looks so good. She's wearing a navy pantsuit, but it's not a downtown business sort of suit. It's more sporty looking. Her shirt is white with narrow red and navy stripes. Her earrings and bracelet match, made of pounded-out gold. Her hair is blonde and comes just below her chin line. She is looking up at my dad like he's the only one in the room.

"You must be Harold!" she says in this bubbly sort of voice, as if she's ready to start laughing in pure joy any minute. "I'm Amy Audet. Isn't it funny how when you talk to someone on the phone, you form a picture in your mind of what they're going to look like? You're not at all what I expected. You're much better looking."

Dad chuckles a bit. I'd never even thought he knew how to chuckle. He's most definitely not the chuckling kind. "Did you imagine I'd be short and fat?" he asks.

"Oh no, of course not," she says. "But I thought you'd be older."

"And I guess I imagined that you'd be shorter and definitely brunette."

My mom's been standing behind me. But now she steps around me and extends her hand to Amy. "I'm Kate," she says. "The owner of half this house, one of the people you'll need to have sign the papers if you're going to get this listing."

Amy turns away from my dad and shakes hands with Mom. "Nice to meet you, Kate. Perhaps you'd like to show me around."

I'm feeling a little embarrassed because it seems to me that Mom isn't being very friendly. Then, as she starts to lead this woman back to the kitchen and family room area, I see Amy look back at my dad and roll her eyes. He just grins back at her. He is not usually the grinning type any more than he's the chuckling type. I think this woman is flirting with him. He probably hasn't noticed. I don't blame Mom for being a bit snippy. It is half her house after all. I'm also thinking Amy Audet is kind of two-faced, which could be a good thing. That way, if I end up hating her for selling our house, I won't feel too guilty.

Knowing that our house will be on the market by next Monday makes me worry that I'm going to be a bag lady. What if Gina's apartment and our house both get sold and Mom still hasn't found a place to rent? She's been looking at ads in the paper for weeks now, but she says everything is too expensive.

I wait until we're eating dinner the next night before telling Mom that I'd like to start walking to the apartment after school instead of going to Grandma's. "That's what I did when I came to visit last Friday, and it worked fine. Why am I going to Grandma's? You have to go way out of your way to pick me up, and I end up almost back where I started in the first place."

"But you've always gone to Grandma's after school. Your dad and I wanted to keep things as normal as possible."

"Well, this doesn't feel very normal to me. Right now I'm bouncing around so much I feel like a ping-pong ball."

"You won't be lonely being on your own every afternoon for that hour or two?"

"I won't be alone. I'll have the dog." I look down at her, sitting by my feet. I slip her a tiny piece of chicken. That's what she's been hoping for. She's becoming a real little bum.

"While we're on the subject of schedules," Mom says, "what are your plans for the weekend?"

"I hadn't thought about it."

"Well, I know you haven't really seen much of your dad this week, but I was hoping you'd spend at least a few hours with me on Saturday."

"Why's that?" I ask.

"I think I've found a place for us to live."

"Really?"

She nods.

"Oh, that's a relief. I was beginning to wonder what was going to happen to us if our house and Gina's apartment sold at the same time."

"The fellow who owns this place is a friend of Ian and Gina's. He's only asking five hundred dollars a month."

"That sounds scary cheap. That's about what they want for those skid row kind of hotel rooms down by the river."

"Well, it is in Langley," she says. "Rents are definitely cheaper there."

"Langley!"

"It will be a longer drive to get to work and to your dad's, but it's not that bad and it's only going to be for a few months. We'll manage."

I stay overnight with Dad on Friday, but Mom picks me up about ten the next morning. While we're driving out to Langley, I ask if she's seen this place yet.

"Yes," she answers, "I was over last night. I've put down a deposit."

"So what's it like?"

"You . . . you've got to understand . . . it's nothing fancy. It's not at all like our house. You might want to think of it as an adventure. It will be like we're going on holiday, like we're going camping."

Like we're camping? I'm beginning to wonder if this place will have a bathroom or if we'll be trudging out to use shared toilets and showers like we did that summer we stayed up at Harrison Lake. Or will the bathroom be like one of those little tiny ones Dad's friend had in his fifth wheeler. Dad said it was so small he could sit on the toilet, wash his hands in the sink, and wash his feet in the shower – all at the same time. He didn't really do that, but he wasn't exaggerating. He could have.

"How much farther do we have to go?" It feels like we've been driving forever.

"Just after that next set of lights," she answers.

As we pass the lights, Mom pulls into the curb lane and starts to slow down. I see the sign ahead. Highland Estates. As soon as we turn into the driveway, I see we're in a trailer park.

Inside the gate, she has to slow right down because there's a bright yellow speed bump. You can see more of them at intervals all down the narrow strip of cracked and potholed pavement ahead.

Mom points to a neat white bungalow with green trim. "That's where the caretakers live," she says.

"So there are real houses as well as trailers in here?"

"They don't call them trailers. They're mobile homes. That's a double wide."

I don't care what she wants to call them. If the place she's rented is anything like this one, it might be okay after all. It has its own little yard bordered by a picket fence. It's pretty much like the place Siobhan's grandma has in the retirement community where she lives. I just hope this doesn't mean everyone here will be old.

As we drive farther in, we pass real trailer-looking trailers: corrugated tin ones with rusty streaks at the seams. One has three old cars in front of it, none with a licence plate. Two of the cars have their hoods up and a man is leaning in to one. He stands up and watches us go by. The good news is that he's not old. He might even be a bit good-looking. It's hard to tell because he's so covered with grease.

"How come they're called mobile homes?" I ask. "They don't look very mobile to me."

All the trailers have add-ons of some sort. There are porches, decks, and lean-tos attached to them. Some have added wood siding and a few even have brick facing.

"Well, they're easier to move than a regular house," Mom answers.

It seems like every second place we see has those icicle-style Christmas lights hanging from the eaves. It's April. "Why do they have Christmas lights up? Even the stores don't put their Christmas stuff up much before Halloween."

"I guess they're just really efficient people," Mom says. "Anyway, here we are."

She's slowed almost to a standstill in front of the weirdest place I've ever seen. It is a single wide trailer that's white on top and red on the bottom. Icicle lights outline the flat roof of the main unit and hang from the eaves of the large covered deck that's attached to one side of it. The lights that edge the eaves of the deck are interspersed with hanging baskets filled with brightly colored plastic flowers. There are two sets of wide steps coming down from the deck. One set is clear for walking, but the other is covered with big and small planters. In some places, they're balanced on top of each other. Some of the vines and greenery that are spilling out of the planters look real; other planters are filled with artificial flowers. The unusual part is that all the planters are shaped like pigs, with holes in their backs for greenery. In front of the trailer, under the big window, there's a shrub about two-and-a-half-feet high and three-feet wide. It's been clipped so that it's shaped like a pig. There's a pig-shaped mailbox and a birdbath with a plastic pig peeing into it. There are brackets supporting trellises on either side of the front window. Each bracket is decorated with a pink wood cutout of a pig. Every window I can see from the road has a stained glass ornament hanging in it. Some of them are too small for me to see clearly from where I am, but want to bet they're all pigs?

Mom has pulled into a spot on the side of the trailer opposite the deck.

"What do you think?" she says.

"Those pigs have got to go," I tell her. "I always thought all those rules they have in Greenwood Glade were a bit much. You know, how we all have to have aggregate driveways, and we can only use certain finishes and colors, and everyone has to have exactly nineteen shrubs. Now I'm beginning to understand. Do they have rules about decorating your whole house with pink pigs?" I just can't see it happening in our subdivision.

"That's Mrs. Warren's place, not ours."

Mom is getting out of the car and I realize that our place is the plain, little, brown and cream trailer next to the pig place. Now that I know how much worse it could be, I'm relieved. This is a trailer, plain and simple. No one's going to think it's a bungalow. I don't think anyone would call it a mobile home either. Still, the guy who owns it has taken down his Christmas lights and any pigs he might have had around the place. There's a small porch at the single door, which is about a third of the way down one side of the trailer. Behind the porch is an unpainted wood lean-to. It has no windows and I can't see a door. Maybe you can only get to it from the inside of the trailer.

Oh please, God, I silently pray. *Don't let that be my bedroom.*

Mom doesn't ask what I think of the new place. For this, I am truly thankful.

"Come have a look," she says. "I have the key."

So he's given her the key. It must really be a done deal; it's probably too late for her to back out.

I follow her up the three steps onto the little porch, testing the railing as I go. It doesn't look all that sturdy. Mom opens the door and stands back so I can go in first. What can I say? It's like walking into the den of some small, burrowing animal. Everything is dark brown. Directly opposite the door is the kitchen sink, set in a row of cupboards done in dark wood. There is no division between this kitchen area and what must be the living room. All the walls are covered in dark wood paneling. There's a pretty big window at the end of the living room and smaller ones over the sink and next to the door where I'm standing, but all the dark wood totally sucks up the light. The rug in the living room is a mottled brown-and-beige mix. The kitchen linoleum is cream-colored with a very busy brown-and-orange pattern. It extends down the hall.

Mom closes the door behind us. It's even darker. I scan the bare room. They've left the fridge and stove. There's no dishwasher. The appliances are baby-poop yellow. I know all about that color because I once started to change the diaper on Siobhan's little sister Erin and found she had this stuff in her Huggies. Totally gross. I thought something must be seriously wrong with her, but Siobhan said it's normal for them to have that yellow poop when they aren't being fed anything but milk. Then she gave me this big lesson on how it gets darker when they start eating solids like meat and vegetables. It was way more than I ever wanted to know about poop, but she was changing the diaper and washing Erin's bum while she talked, so mostly I was just glad she was such an expert and had taken over. I'd sincerely hoped I'd never see anything like that again. Now here I am with that color being the only bright spot in the trailer.

"The bedrooms are down this way," Mom says, steering me to the left down a narrow hall. The first room on the right is the bathroom. It's a normal size, but it looks smaller because it too is paneled in dark wood. The fixtures are that poopy-yellow color again.

Mom notices me looking at them.

"That color is harvest gold," she says. "It was very big in the late sixties and early seventies. Did you notice the fridge and stove are the same color? It's sort of retro."

That's not the word I'd use.

The next door leads to a tiny bedroom. I won't even talk about the paneling. It's in every single room. It's especially awful in such a little room with only one small window.

The hall ends at a larger bedroom. Same walls, and it looks like they've used some of the leftover carpet from the living room. It's the same color and pattern, but it doesn't quite cover the whole floor and the edges are all frayed.

"Of course, we'll fix it up a bit. You remember what our house was like when we first moved in." I can tell my mother is trying hard to be cheerful.

She has a point. Like Dad says, anyone who thinks you can't make a silk purse out of a sow's ear has never met my mom. She's really good at fixing places up. When people see our house, they always think we're kind of rich, which we're not. Dad and Mom got our place cheap because the people who owned it before us didn't make their mortgage payments and the bank foreclosed. Then the bank had trouble selling it because the house hadn't been kept up very well. You wouldn't know it was the same house now. So maybe Mom's right. Maybe she can make this place nice too, or at least nicer. Anything's bound to be an improvement.

"It will be a challenge," I say.

"What colors would you like in your room?"

"What would go with all that wood?"

"Oh, I thought we'd paint over it, but if you like the wood, we can . . ."

"No, no. Paint sounds good."

We haven't been in the trailer long, but there isn't much to see, so we lock up and head back to Surrey. She's going to drop me off at Dad's. It's a quiet ride.

Dad's home when we get there. He says he has things to discuss with Mom. I go upstairs because I just want to be alone anyway. I look around my bedroom. When Dad and Mom were fixing it up last spring, Dad took the doors off one of my closets and made it into a study nook. I can't remember if my new bedroom even has a closet. It must. It's probably disguised. Press one of the wood panels and it will give way to reveal . . . a wood paneled closet.

Siobhan comes over to visit later in the afternoon and I tell her about our new place.

"And how do you feel about that?" she asks in that kind of phony voice our school counselor, Mrs. Blanchard, always uses.

"Well, it will be a relief to settle a bit and lose this crazy schedule I've been on."

"But it's in Langley."

"There's nothing wrong with Langley."

"But it's so far away. My mom won't ever want to drive me there to visit."

"You can still visit me when I'm at my dad's," I say.

"Yeah, but what about when your house is sold?"

"We can visit at his new place. He'll have to get an apartment or something, and I'm sure he wouldn't mind coming to get you."

"If he has half a brain, he'll get a place in Vancouver or Burnaby so he doesn't have that three hours of commuting every day."

I hadn't thought of that, but she's right. It would make more sense for him to live closer to his work.

"Well, my mom will drive me to your house," I say. "And it's not like we'll be living there for long. It's just temporary."

"And how are you going to get to school?" she asks. "Your grandma's not going to want to drive all the way to Langley to get you."

"No one would even think of asking her to do that. I'll manage on my own. I can take the bus, like you do."

Siobhan catches the school bus at Sacred Heart, the elementary school that's only two blocks from her house. "Do they have a school bus coming in from Langley?" she asks.

"They must. I'll get Mom to check where I have to go to catch it." I'm trying to sound really confident and sure of myself as I explain things to Siobhan, but she's got me a bit worried. I wonder if Mom has thought of any of this. I decide to call her Sunday night to ask her to check where I have to go to catch the bus from Langley to Holy Name.

It's the first thing I ask about when she gets back to the apartment Monday after work.

"Have you walked the dog?" she asks.

"Yes, of course. First thing, like she gave me any choice." I try to sound stern, but I don't do a good job of it. The dog is finally over that crazy spell she had when I first came in, and now she's sleeping. Guess where? On my lap. She thinks she owns me.

"But about the school bus . . ."

"Why don't I get dinner together first," she says. "Then we can have a real talk about it."

Why does this reply make me feel uneasy? She doesn't have to draw me a map. I just want to know if the school bus leaves from somewhere I can walk to or if I'll maybe have to take a city bus to hook up with it. I've never taken a city bus, but how hard can it be?

She keeps me hanging until we're finished eating and then she drops the bomb. "I called the school today," she says. "There is no bus in from Langley. Their buses leave from Sacred Heart in Surrey and from Our Lady of the Sea in White Rock. That's it."

I'm trying to think of a Plan B. "Well, could you drop me off on your way to work?"

"It would mean you'd get to school at eight o'clock."

"That would be okay. I could go to mass before school started." I like the idea. Grandma would be really impressed, and if I was that holy, maybe God would listen to me for a change and my mom and dad would get back together again. I'm thinking I should pray that they buy another house close to Siobhan's when they get back together.

"It's the afternoons that won't work," Mom's saying. "I'm not off till four-thirty and traffic is bad by then. I wouldn't be able to pick you up till five."

"If I have to wait, I have to wait."

"They're not running a babysitting service there, Lucy. They clear that school and lock up the doors as soon as any after-school games are finished. Remember the time you forgot your library book in your locker and we went back to get it?"

I do. We had to run around knocking on one door after another. They were all locked and no one heard us. Finally, Mom saw a custodian working in a class-room and went up and knocked on the window.

"Poor Grandma," I say. "It will be such a long drive for her, and I suppose she'll get caught up in rush hour after she drops me off and starts back home."

"What are you talking about?" Mom yells. "You leave your grandmother out of this."

"Well, how else am I supposed to get home?"

"How could you even think of asking her? And don't bother trying to do it behind my back. Even if she agrees, I won't let her do it."

"You don't have to have a fit about it," I say. "You don't like my idea, so fine. Do you have a better one?"

"There's a public high school just a few blocks down the road from the trailer park. The only plan that makes sense is for you to finish the school year there."

At first, I am totally speechless. I won't know a single person. I've never been to a public school. I start to cry. "I'll get pregnant, just like you did. I don't want to be a mother when I'm fourteen."

My mother rolls her eyes. "So Grandma's managed to blame that on the public schools?"

"She said the supervision on the ski trip you went on wasn't good enough."

"So you won't go on any ski trips, okay?"

"But I won't know anyone there."

"You'll meet other kids. Maybe you'll even make friends with someone who lives close by. Think how nice that would be. You and Siobhan never see as much of each other as you'd like because you live so far apart and have to wait till someone's free to give you a ride. Think what it would be like to have a friend to walk to school with each day."

I try to imagine meeting someone new who would want to be this kind of friend. I can't.

"Once the house sells, I'll have more money," she says. "And I'll start looking for another place in Surrey. Hopefully you'll be back at Holy Name by September. This is just temporary."

It seems like everything in my life is temporary these days.

"And public school will be a good experience for you. You'll have all sorts of adventures to tell Siobhan about."

Right. I read the papers. I'll get to learn about putting condoms on bananas. I'm sure Siobhan's mother will be real happy if I start teaching Siobhan stuff like that.

That night, I lie awake tossing and turning. I have to come up with a plan. In the morning, I call Grandma and tell her I really need to see a priest. I want her to pick me up after school. If she'll drive me to Saint Francis, I can walk back to her place after I'm finished my appointment.

Grandma is too good a Catholic to say no or to ask why I need to talk to a priest. She probably thinks I've committed a really bad sin. If I had and she didn't help me get to confession right away, I might get hit by a truck and go to hell and it would all be her fault. So she just says sure, she'll pick me up from school.

Then I call Mom and tell her I want to visit Grandma this afternoon. Mom says she'll come and get me there when she's finished work.

Grandma picks me up after school and drops me off in front of the church about three-thirty. I go into the parish office. The lady at the desk looks like she's been sucking lemons. She eyes me up and down. I'm wearing my school uniform. I'm not one of those girls who roll up the waistband of the kilt to make it shorter. I look like a good Catholic girl, I'm sure of it.

"Do you have an appointment?" she asks.

I shake my head no.

"Both Father Mac and Father Tony are very busy," she says. "They don't have time to just chat with visitors."

"Excuse me? I didn't come here just to chat . . ." I don't get to finish my sentence.

"Lucy!" Father Tony says. "I'm so glad you dropped by."

I was actually hoping to talk to Father Mac because he at least has some manners. He'd never tell me I looked like a dog. Still, Father Tony is better than old prune-face here.

I follow him down a long hall to his office. When we get there, he leaves the door partway open.

"I've come to talk to you about personal matters," I say. "Shouldn't we close the door?"

He opens it wider. "From my desk, I'll be able to see if anyone comes near enough to hear," he says.

I guess that's okay. "It's about my parents and about school," I tell him.

He makes a little tent with his fingers and waits.

"You probably didn't know, but my mom and dad have split up."

"Actually, I did know. Your dad and I have talked about it."

"Well, I was going to stay with Dad, but he works too late at night and so he can't really look after me."

He nods.

"So I'm going to have to live with Mom, but she has hardly any money and the only place she could afford to rent is in Langley."

"That's a long way from your friends, isn't it?"

I just nod. No need to tell him I really only have one friend. "The thing is, though, they don't have a bus from Langley to Holy Name, so Mom wants me to finish the school year in a public school."

He doesn't look as worried as I thought he would.

"My faith is very important to me; I don't think it's a good idea for me to be going to a public school where they teach you to put condoms on bananas and don't even allow you to pray."

A funny look comes over Father Tony's face. He puts his elbow on his desk and props his chin up with his hand, half covering his mouth.

"The thing is, Mom could drop me off at Holy Name on her way to work. That way, I'd get to go to mass every day. I think that would be very good for my spiritual growth."

He lowers his forearm down to the desk and I can see that he's been smiling. I imagine it makes a priest happy to learn that a person is serious about her religion and wants to be really holy.

"The problem is with after school. Mom couldn't pick me up till five o'clock and that's too late. I'm sure my grandma would come and get me, but Mom says I'm not supposed to ask her. She says, even if Grandma agrees to it, Mom won't let her."

"How old is your grandma?"

"She's way older than you'd expect. Sixty-seven, I think. She didn't get married till she was thirty-six."

"So your mom is maybe worried about her taking on too much?"

"I don't see why. I mean, Grandma's blood pressure gets a little out of hand sometimes, but usually she's pretty healthy. Anyway, I was thinking that maybe you could have a talk with her and Mom. You know, explain to them how they have a duty to make sure I have a Catholic education. I think they'd listen to a priest."

He sits there looking at his hands for a second or two. "I don't think that would be a wise thing for me to do, Lucy. I'm sure I could persuade your grandma. You could do that yourself, couldn't you?"

I nod.

"The problem would be your mother. I don't think she'd listen to me. She'd just be mad at me for interfering."

I feel deflated. Especially because I know he's probably right.

"I don't think you need to worry about losing your faith even if you do go to a public school for a couple of months. Lots of very devout Catholics have done all their schooling in the public system." He must see how sad I look because he carries on and says, "Look, I'll tell you what I will do. I'll have a talk with Sister Cecile. I suspect that there are other students who attend Holy Cross but live in Langley. They'll have made some sort of transportation arrangement. Maybe we can get you a ride with one of them."

I smile for the first time since I've come in. I hadn't even thought of that. I walk out of there feeling like the problem's finally solved.

I'm wrong. A few days later, I'm in homeroom when my name is called over the intercom. I'm supposed to go to the office. Sister Cecile wants to see me. She couldn't be nicer about it, but that doesn't help when it's all bad news. There are three kids from our school who come in from Langley each day. Their parents take turns driving. The problem is, they'd have to backtrack and go really far out of their way to come pick me up.

"I can get a ride in with my mom," I say. "It's a way *home* that I need. They could just drop me off at a bus stop on their way home and then maybe I could get a city bus to my place."

"Have you ever ridden a city bus?" Sister Cecile asks.

"No, but I'm sure I could figure it out."

"Well, it was Mrs. Dejarlais and Mrs. Murphy I was talking to. I'll call them again and see what they think of that plan. You need to check out the bus routes and find a drop-off place that would work for you."

After I leave the office, I head back to class, but all I can think about is going to the library to use the computers to look up bus schedules online. I'm so pre-occupied I don't even hear Sister Alexis when she asks me a question in class. She gives me a warning. If she catches me daydreaming again, I'll have to write an essay for her. I've heard some of the really horrible topics she picks for punishment essays, so I work hard at paying attention until the bell finally rings.

When lunchtime comes, I don't bother eating. I go straight to the library.

It takes me awhile, but Ms. Renaud, the librarian, and I finally figure out how to use the bus company's Web site. If you put in the starting address and the destination address, it tells you what bus to take. I wonder where these other kids live. The Willow Brook Mall is pretty much in the center of town, and there's a bus that goes from there right past the entrance to our trailer park. I wonder if Mrs. Dejarlais or Mrs. Murphy could drop me off at the mall.

I'm waiting for Sister Cecile when she gets back from lunch.

"I checked the buses," I say. "I can get one from the Willow Brook Mall right to my door. Is the Willow Brook Mall on their route home?"

"I don't know, Lucy," she says. "I told Mrs. Murphy about your suggestion, and she said she'd talk to Mrs. Dejarlais about it. She called back just before lunch, and they both feel very uncomfortable about dropping you off at a mall or at some bus stop on the highway. They'd feel responsible for you if anything went wrong and you didn't get home safely."

"So what does that mean?"

"They feel badly about it, but they're going to have to turn you down."

It takes every ounce of strength I have not to burst into tears right there in the principal's office. I'm halfway out the door before I remember to thank Sister Cecile for trying. It's not her fault it didn't work out. I guess it's not anyone's fault.

I'm a total zombie all afternoon. It's not until fifth period that I come up with a new plan. I'll just have to use the city buses.

As soon as the final bell rings, I head back to the library. I look up the bus company Web site again. It will plan my trip for me. All I have to do is put in the address of my school and the address of the trailer park – and voilà! I get a map and a list of all the buses I have to take.

I head out the front doors of the school and walk down to One-hundred-and-sixtieth Street. It is pouring rain and I forgot my umbrella, but I'm not too worried. There's a bus shelter. There are a couple of other kids wearing Holy Name uniforms who are already waiting. I check my instructions. I need the 335 Fleetwood bus. When it pulls up, I have my money ready and I drop it into the box as I get on. I start to walk down the aisle to find a seat.

"Do you need a transfer?" asks a girl's voice from behind me.

I don't know what she's talking about. I can see she's glancing down at the instruction sheet in my hand.

"Are you going to be taking another bus after this one?" she asks.

"Yeah, I have to take three of them," I answer.

"Ask for a transfer," she says. "Otherwise you'll have to pay again when you get on your next bus."

I don't have to ask for a transfer. The bus driver must have heard the girl because he just hands me one.

I find a seat and the girl who helped me with the transfer sits down next to me.

"You don't happen to be going to Langley, by any

chance?" I ask. It would sure be a lot easier if I could tag along with someone who knew the system.

"No, I'm getting off at Fraser Highway."

"I've never tried riding the buses before," I say.

"Where are you going?"

I hand her my trip plan.

"You sure picked a complicated trip to start with," she says. "But you're changing buses at Fraser Highway, so you'll be getting off at the same stop as me."

At least that's a help. She also shows me where I'm supposed to wait for my next bus.

"Do I put this transfer in the coin box when I get on?" I ask her.

"No. Just show it to the driver and keep hold of it. You'll need it again when you get to Langley Centre."

I have a half hour wait. It seems longer than that. The bus shelter doesn't help when the wind is blowing the rain right into it. I'm soaked. When the bus finally arrives, it's so full I can't get a seat. I try to hang onto one of the straps, but I'm too short to get my hand through it. Eventually, I just grab the back of one of the seats. Every time the bus stops or turns a corner, I just about go flying. The ride goes on forever. My feet are cold and wet. If I wiggle my toes, I can feel the water squishing up between them. Finally, we get to Langley Centre, which is a big bus loop. It seems like everyone is getting off at once. I almost get trampled.

Once I get onto the pavement, I start looking for Bay 4. I check my schedule. I have another half hour wait. It's still raining and windy. The bus shelter at Bay 4 is full of people. I have to stand in the open. Buses are coming and going, and one pulls right up next to me, spraying water all down my left side. I wonder what time it is. This is taking way longer than I expected. I thought I'd be able to make my trip and still get home before Mom, but it's almost five o'clock and I still have one more bus to take.

I find a pay phone and call home. She isn't in yet, so I leave a message. I tell her to pick me up in front of our trailer park. I say I should be there in about half an hour. Then I go back and wait some more. People are forming lines. When the C63 bus comes in, it's already half full. Everyone starts pushing toward it, and before I even get close, the driver closes the doors. The bus is full.

I'm totally panicking. "What do I do now?" I ask the woman in front of me.

She shrugs. "We'll just have to wait for the next one."

"And how long will that be?" I ask.

"About half an hour."

It's the longest half hour of my life. Finally, our bus arrives. This time I get on; I even get a seat.

The route this bus takes jigs and jogs all over the place. At every stop, it seems like more people get on; no one is getting off. I start to worry. I've only been to this trailer park once before, and it's not like I was paying much attention to the route. How will I know where to get off?

I get out of my seat and make my way up to the

driver. The next time he stops at a light, I tell him where I'm going and ask where I should get off. He says at the intersection of Two-hundredth and Twenty-fourth. He'll call out the stop just before we get there. I go back to my place, but this guy with a shaved head and a lot of tattoos has taken my seat. I hang onto the back of it and try to pierce the guy's bald head with my steely glare.

The driver calls my stop and I'm barely down the steps before I hear my mom yelling. Her car is parked on the other side of the road, but she's gotten out and is heading for me. For a wild minute, I think about climbing back onto the bus. She looks that mad.

"What possessed you!" she yells. "I've been worried sick. I have your granddad out looking for you. Your dad's on his way home so he can help."

"But I left you a message."

"Yes, and you said you'd be here at five-thirty." She's waving her arm in front of me, pointing at her watch. "It's 6:25!" she says.

"Well, one of the buses was full, so I had to wait for the next one."

"And how am I supposed to know that? You've never been on a bus before. You could easily have made a wrong connection. I had no idea where you were."

She's soaked and her hair is all frizzled. Mine is hanging in clumps, and water is dripping off all the pointy ends. I'm shivering.

"Shouldn't we get in the car?" I ask.

Mom turns around and stomps back to it. She stops at the first gas station we come to on the way back to Surrey and she uses the pay phone to call Grandma and Dad. After that, she doesn't say a word until we're almost home. By then, the car heater has warmed me up and I'm feeling almost human.

"Lucy, just don't ever do anything like that again, you understand? You really scared me."

She doesn't have to worry. I'm feeling so stupid. My trip plan is a soggy mess in my hands, but now I see that it says right at the top that my arrival time would be 5:46. I was so busy concentrating on getting to the right buses, all I worried about was whether I'd be on time to catch them.

"I won't," I say. "It seemed like a good plan at the time. I thought I'd be able to show you I could take the bus home from school."

"You showed me all right."

"I wouldn't want to do it again anyway. It took me almost three hours, and it was a totally miserable trip."

It's seven o'clock when we get home. Lucky me, I get through the door first. The dog is frantic, but before I can even bend down to pat her, the smell hits me. Mom turns on the light. I look down at the floor. The dog's had an accident. I've just stepped in it.

"Put on a pair of my boots and take the dog out," Mom says. Her teeth are clenched. I think it would be a good idea for both the dog and me to get out of her way for awhile. We take a long walk.

By the time we get back, Mom has cleaned up the mess and heated up some soup. I take off her boots and she throws a couple of cheese sandwiches on the stove.

"I'm so sorry," I say. "I didn't ever think I'd cause this much trouble."

Mom shrugs. "Part of it's my fault. I knew the dog had been cooped up all day. I should have taken her with me. I could have walked her while I was waiting for you. I was just in such a panic I wasn't thinking straight."

She puts her hands on my shoulders and leans her forehead against mine. After a second, she says, "I get first dibs on that bathtub!" she says.

"That's okay. I can wait till I get to Dad's."

"Oh," she says, "I told him you might as well spend the night here. He brought a pile of work home with him anyway."

That's fine by me.

eight

The next day, I'm telling Siobhan and Mariah about my horrible bus trip and how it seems that there's no way I can stay at Holy Name, that I'm going to have to go to Carey High near the trailer park.

"I bet the public school won't be all that different," Mariah says. "Just no religion classes. Will you still go to church?"

"Of course," I answer. "Just because I live too far away to get to a Catholic high school doesn't mean I'm turning into a godless heathen."

"I didn't mean it that way . . ."

"Well, I should hope not."

"I wish I could go to the public school," Siobhan says.

"Why?"

"I'd really like to lose this uniform."

I haven't even thought about that part. "I don't know what I'll wear. Probably I'll put on the wrong thing and everyone will think I'm a geek." It's one more thing for me to worry about.

"I know what I'd wear," says Siobhan.

"I can just guess: a short skirt and a plunging neckline to show off your boobs."

She looks offended. "You're just jealous because you don't have any."

I don't even bother replying. Mom and I are moving on Friday, so this will be my last week in school with Siobhan. I don't want to end up having a fight with her.

It's a good thing that I don't, because she can be very nice sometimes.

On my last day, just as we're finishing lunch, she says she has to get something from her locker. We're sitting at a table with a bunch of the other girls from our class, and when she leaves, they all start acting a bit weird. They keep looking toward the door she went through, then exchanging sideways glances.

A few minutes later, Siobhan comes back, carrying a cake tin with a plastic lid. She sets it down in front of me, and everyone yells, "Surprise!"

She takes the lid off.

The cake has cream-colored icing and she's drawn a face on it. The eyes are outlined in brown icing, but the irises are filled in green, like my eyes. The mouth is pink and sad. She has made blue tears below the eyes.

I take one look at it and start to cry.

Siobhan's face falls. "It's supposed to make you feel better," she says. "I made it myself. I thought you'd like it."

"I love it," I say between sobs. "It's a beautiful cake. You're the best friend in the world."

"Hey! A cake! Do we get some?" Jason has come up behind us and is looking over my shoulder.

Siobhan jumps. He shouldn't sneak up on her like that. Brad and Thomas are there too. The three of them always hang together. I keep my face turned from them and wipe my eyes and nose on a napkin so they won't see I've been crying. I don't have to worry. No one notices me. They're all busy talking.

"Siobhan baked Lucy a good-bye cake," says Mariah.

"You baked it yourself?" Jason asks. He's smiling at Siobhan, and I can almost see her heart beating right through her shirt. She has a major crush on him. She says she doesn't, but her blushing and giggling are a dead giveaway.

"I'm a multitalented girl," she says. "If the three of you behave, we might even let you have a piece." She doesn't have to offer twice.

"Cool, I'll get a knife and plates," Jason says, and he heads off to find them.

When he gets back, he hands Siobhan the knife, and she starts cutting the cake. The boys are hanging over the table like a flock of vultures. Who's this cake for anyway? I don't appreciate these guys barging in.

Siobhan gives me the first piece. "This is for Lucy, who we're going to majorly miss."

Then she cuts pieces for the other girls and for Jason and his friends. The boys' pieces are bigger than mine, but I don't get time to worry about how unfair that is because Jason holds up his piece of cake and says, "To Lucy!"

All the kids hold up their pieces of cake like they're toasting me. I almost start crying again.

nine

I stay with Dad on Friday night and all day Saturday because Mom's busy moving and I'd just be in the way. After mass on Sunday, Dad and I go out for lunch. It's about one-thirty when we drive through the gates of Highland Estates. When we get to the trailer, the only car parked by it is a red Miata. I know that car. It belongs to Gina. Sure enough, she opens the door of the trailer and comes out onto the little porch before I even get out of the car.

"Where's Mom?"

"She'll be back in a minute," Gina says. "She's gone with her landlord and his friend to pick up the couch. They have a truck."

We're still standing there talking about it when a big Dodge Ram pulls up. There are two guys in the front seat. They pull ahead of our trailer and start to back into the space next to the door on the side. Dad's car is

in the way. I can see Mom looking out the back window of the crew cab.

"Harold, they need to swing the truck in here," says Gina.

"Yeah, well, I'll be on my way then. See you next Saturday, Lucy." He puts the van in gear and backs out.

As soon as the truck is parked near the trailer, the two guys jump out. One, the cute guy I saw working on the car the first day I came here with Mom, pulls his seat forward and helps Mom out. It's a big jump for her. Then he and the guy who was driving start unloading a couch off the back of the truck. The pattern is orange and gold flowers against a cream background. There's a chair to go with it.

"A Sally Ann special," Mom says. She's come over to stand by me, and we're watching the men wrestle the couch up the stairs and through the door of the trailer.

Just as the two men come out to get the chair off the truck, Mom's car pulls up. Ian gets out of it and reaches into the back seat for the very big case of beer he has there. I don't know why he's driving Mom's car. I'm about to ask when I see Dad's car coming back. There's no room for him to park, but it doesn't matter because he's not staying. He just stops his van in front of the trailer and leaves the motor running.

"You forgot your homework." He hands me my backpack.

"Thanks," I say.

He's not even looking at me. He's watching Mom and Gina and the two guys who are carrying the chair now. When he notices Ian and the big case of beer, he frowns. "Looks like they're planning a party," he says to no one in particular. Then he drives off again without even saying good-bye.

Dad's not the only one who's noticed the activity. I see someone peeking out the window of the pig trailer.

We go inside. Mom is telling the men where to put the couch and chair – not that there are a lot of choices. There's only one wall in the living room area that is long enough for the couch. I look around. The orange and gold flowers of the couch fabric go pretty well with the brown paneled walls, the brown carpet, and the grungy gold fridge and stove. Today, Mom's also somehow come up with a coffee table and two end tables that are wood patterned but definitely not wood. The end tables are two tiered. On the top of one is a brown wood lamp with a bright orange shade. There's a twenty-one-inch TV in the corner and a table with an Arborite top and chrome legs right next to the door we've come in.

When the chair and couch are where Mom wants them, she and Gina stand back to have a look.

"Very retro," says Gina.

"Depressing," says Mom. "But it won't be for long. Come see your room, Lucy. It's a bit better."

I follow her down the hall. I'm afraid to look. She opens the door.

"Ta-da!"

She has painted over the paneling and the room is now a very pale yellow. There is a single bed and the spread has a design of small blue and yellow flowers against a white background. Mom has made curtains of the same material and hung them so they extend over part of the wall on either side of the window, which makes the window look bigger than it is. The poufed valence is blue and matches the flowers in the print. There's a white wicker chair and a small white dresser.

"There's not enough room for a desk," she says. "I guess you'll have to use the kitchen table to do your homework."

"Where will I put my computer?"

"I think you should probably leave it at your dad's," she says. "I don't have internet access here anyway. I can't afford it."

I realize from the tone of her voice that she's still feeling bad. I look around the room again. There's no TV either.

"It's sure a lot cheerier than it was when I saw it last time, isn't it? Neat what you did with the window."

She smiles. "You really think so?"

"Definitely."

There's a lot of noise coming from the kitchen and living room area. Gina, Ian, and the two guys are sitting around the kitchen table. Each of them has an open beer. Of course, the dog is there too. She is running around like she doesn't know what to do with herself.

She's going to get stepped on if she doesn't smarten up. This trailer isn't big enough for three full-grown men. It feels way too crowded.

As soon as we come into the room, one of the men stands up to let Mom have his chair. No one even bothers to introduce me.

"Sit down, Randy," says my mom. "I'm going to make some sandwiches. Lucy, come give me a hand, will you?"

We use up a whole loaf of bread making sandwiches. I spread the butter, mustard, and mayo. Mom piles on meat, cheese, and lettuce. By the time we get them to the table, everyone's having a second beer. They're very noisy. I can tell it's upsetting the dog. No one is paying any attention to her.

I'm not hungry. I decide the dog would probably be happier somewhere quiet. I pick her up, planning to take her to my room.

"Oh, Lucy, thanks so much," says Gina. "Kate, where's Lucy's leash?"

"Oh, are you going to take her for a walk?" Mom asks. "She'll appreciate that. She hasn't been out since first thing this morning."

I had not planned to take the dog for a walk. If she hasn't been out since this morning, she's sure going to need to poop soon. Why should this be my responsibility when Gina is just sitting around drinking beer? But I'm standing with the leash in my hands, and the dog isn't smart enough to know what I'm thinking, so she's on her hind legs, twirling around in front of me like a ballerina. How can I say no? I snap the leash to her collar and head for the door.

"Don't forget a baggy," Mom says. She hands me one.

We walk around the trailer park. There's a community hall in the middle of it and a tiny park behind that. I'm heading in that direction, but then I see three girls sitting at a picnic table there, smoking cigarettes. They look older than me, but probably not by that much. I don't know what I'd say to them if I went that way, so I turn right and walk down a different lane. It's maybe ten minutes later that I get home again, proudly carrying my plastic bag of dog poop. I hope everyone's happy.

They certainly sound that way. Ian is telling jokes. Everyone is laughing except my mom, who just looks tired.

I take the dog to my bedroom with me. I leave the door open a bit, and when I see my mom passing by on her way to the bathroom, I call to her. "We're going to get kicked out of this place the same day we moved in," I say as she stands in my doorway. "They're being so noisy. What will your landlord say?"

"Randy *is* the landlord."

"Who's Randy?"

"The guy with the blond hair. The one with the ponytail."

I'm stunned. "You pay him rent and everything?"

She nods and then says she really has to go to the bathroom. When she leaves, she closes my door behind her. The dog and I are glad. We can use what little privacy we can get.

The bunch of them carry on partying in our kitchen all afternoon. I wander out of my room a little after five o'clock. There's no sign of dinner. There are still some sandwiches left. I take a couple from the plate and find a can of pop in the fridge. I go back to my room. I share the sandwiches with the dog. She likes the ham and cheese, but she won't eat the lettuce.

Everyone finally leaves about eight o'clock. I still have the dog. Gina didn't even come to say good-bye to her. I can hear Mom moving around in the kitchen, then her steps pass my bedroom door and I hear her turn on the shower. A few minutes later, she sticks her head into my room. "It's been a really busy weekend, Lucy. I'm going to call it a night."

It's eight-thirty. She never goes to bed this early. I wonder how much beer she's had.

After Mom's asleep, I call Siobhan and tell her all about it. "The first day we move in and here she is having this big drinking party. What do you think of that?"

"It doesn't sound good," says Siobhan.

I agree.

"But moving is really stressful, and if all those

people were helping her, maybe she felt she had to give them a beer and a bit of something to eat."

"I could understand if she'd given each of them one beer, but she had Ian buy a whole case, one of the big ones. It had fifteen bottles of beer in it, and they drank them all!"

"Well, at least your mom was alone when she went to bed."

I'm confused. "What does that have to do with how much beer they all drank?"

"My parents always say that if they didn't drink so much, they'd have a way smaller family."

"You're joking!"

"No, it's that way with lots of people. Drinking gives them ideas."

I start wondering about this landlord of ours. I hope he isn't going to be bringing beer over all the time. And what about Jake? That's the name of the other guy, the one who was working on his car the first day I came to see the place. How did Mom meet him? What was he doing here tonight? I wonder if I really should visit Dad on the weekends. Maybe I should stay here and keep an eye out for Mom. I definitely don't want her getting ideas like the ones Siobhan's parents get.

"Maybe we should join Alateen," Siobhan says.

"What's Alateen?"

"Mariah goes. They meet in the basement at Saint Ignatius every Friday night. It's for teenagers whose parents are alcoholics."

"Do you think my mom's an alcoholic?"

Until the last two weeks, I'd never seen her drink anything except a glass of wine with dinner. Even that was only on very special occasions. Now, all of a sudden, she's guzzling beer.

"Mariah has this sort of test," says Siobhan. "I'll get it for you. But she says it doesn't matter if your parent is a real alcoholic. The club is for any teen who's being affected by a parent's drinking."

"Like having to spend all day in my room to get away from the noisy party?"

"Yeah, like that. I'm sure they'd let us join. And it's on a Friday night, so you'll be staying at your dad's place. It will be cool. That way, even though you have to go to a new school, at least we'll get to see each other once a week."

I like the sound of that.

Monday morning, I'm not worrying about my mom's drinking anymore because I have bigger problems. I'm so stressed about my first day at this new school that I'm a total wreck.

"What am I supposed to wear?"

Mom and I stand in my room, looking into the pokey little closet. It isn't crowded. When you wear the same old uniform for school every day, you don't need many clothes.

"Probably jeans and any top you want would be fine," Mom says.

I put on the clothes I'd wear if I were going to Siobhan's on a Saturday. Trouble is, I look like I'm about ten.

"The school is close enough that you can walk," Mom says. "This will be quite handy."

"I'm not walking."

"But if I drive you, you'll get there way earlier than you need to."

"I have too much stuff to carry."

So she drives me to school and takes me up to the office. The school is horrible. The place is huge. The kids are huge. It's not like going to high school with all your friends from elementary. There's no orientation where everyone is really nice and shows you around. The secretary takes me in to see the counselor.

The counselor doesn't seem all that friendly. She just works out a timetable for me. Then she finds me a locker, and when I have my books sorted out, she takes me to the class that's going to be my homeroom. The teacher is a man. She introduces us. I forget his name the second she says it. I can't remember the counselor's name either. It's still early. I'm the only kid in the classroom.

The teacher shows me to a seat and then goes back to the marking he was doing when I came in. I sit there and try to pray. Where's God when you need Him?

I'm there maybe five or ten minutes when the bell rings. Kids start pouring into the room. They're all talking at once. A lot of them have drinks or are eating something. There's lots of pushing and shoving. At first, no one even notices me.

Then this one guy looks at me and says, "Hey, Babe, wrong class."

That catches the attention of some other kids. A big girl with the world's shortest skirt and black- and blue-striped hair says, "Wrong school, honey. The elementary's two blocks over."

She and her friends laugh. The teacher is telling them all to sit down. It takes forever, but finally things are quiet enough that he can introduce me. I feel like a specimen. He points at me and tells everyone my name. They're supposed to make me feel welcome. Good luck. Of course, he doesn't tell me their names – not that I could begin to remember them. No one even says hi.

The teacher takes roll call and reads some announcements. The bell rings again.

Chaos breaks out. Everyone is talking and jostling. I don't know where I'm going, so I just sit there. The room has almost emptied, but I see one girl who seems to be hanging back.

Finally, she comes over to me. "What class do you have first?" she asks.

"Science," I say. "Room 216."

"Follow me."

I do. She's an Indo-Canadian girl with hair down past her butt. I don't think she's really had a proper look at me yet. Any time I look at her, she looks down right away. She's really shy, I think. I don't know where

I'm going and I don't know this girl's name, but what do I have to lose? I couldn't be any more lost with her than I would be on my own.

The class she leads me to has high benches and stools instead of desks and chairs. The posters on the walls list all the safety rules you're supposed to follow when you're working in the lab. Definitely a science class. I smile my thanks.

"You can sit here," she says, pointing to a stool.

When the teacher comes in, my new friend calls her over. "This is Lucy. She just moved here."

The friendly girl makes sure I get to all my morning classes, and she sits down at an empty table with me at lunch.

"You know how you introduced me to all the teachers?" I ask.

"Yeah," she says without raising her eyes from the lunch bag she's just opened.

"Well, there's one important person you forgot to introduce."

She looks up at me, all worried. Then she looks around the cafeteria.

"Who?"

"You."

She's been so serious all morning, but suddenly her face lights up in a smile. "I'm Harbie. Harbie Grewal," she says.

Another girl comes up to our table, carrying a tray. She looks at me, and for a second, it's like she can't decide whether to sit down or not. Harbie looks up from her lunch and sees her.

"Kuldeep, this is Lucy."

The girl nods at me. She sits down next to Harbie.

"Lucy just moved here," Harbie says.

"Where from?" Kuldeep asks.

"From Surrey," I say. "I used to go to Holy Name."

Kuldeep nods again.

We compare timetables. Kuldeep will be in my art class, which I have right after lunch. She says she'll show me how to get there.

They don't talk much, but they're friendly, and I'm thinking this might all work out. Then four boys approach the table. They just stand there beside us, looking me over.

"You the new girl?" one of them finally asks.

I nod.

He shrugs and smirks at his friends. Then he looks back at me. "We always have to check out any new girls. Hoped you might be a hottie." And just like that, they all walk away.

I *am* a hottie. My face is so hot I'm surprised I haven't set off the sprinkler system.

I look at Harbie. She just shrugs.

"Why do I feel so insulted?" I ask. "I don't want to be a hottie."

"Probably don't want to be treated like a piece of meat either," Kuldeep says. Then she takes another bite from her sandwich.

*

All things considered, it isn't such a bad first day. I stand in front of the school for a minute or two after I come out, waiting. Then I remember I'm on my own. I have a key to our trailer, and I have responsibilities at home.

The first thing I do when I get there is take the dog for a walk. It's not like I have much choice. It's either that or feed her valium. When she's all happy and calmed down, I walk her home, get comfortable on the couch, and call Grandma. While I'm talking to her, I get up to get a cola from the fridge. As I head back to the couch, I see the girl from my homeroom class, the one with the black and blue hair and the skirt up to her crotch who told me to go find the elementary school. She's walking by, almost under our front window. She must live in the trailer park.

I tell Grandma about the girl. I'm wondering now if she was one of that group I saw smoking down at the park the day we moved in. Grandma doesn't think I should go out of my way to make friends with her. I don't think Grandma has much to worry about.

ten

By the end of our first week in the trailer, I'm pretty sure I won't have to go to Alateen. There are no more noisy parties. None of the men come over with cases of beer. It's just me, Mom, and the dog. It can't be too exciting to watch us, but that's what the lady who lives in the pig house does. She must spend all day sitting at her window.

Friday morning, I'm just coming back from walking the dog when she comes out onto her deck. I'd have expected her to be plump and pink, but she's skinny and everything about her looks gray. Her hair is tightly permed and reminds me of steel wool pads. Her face is wrinkled and ashen. She's clutching at the gray cardigan that she's wearing over what I think is her nightgown. She's smoking a cigarette.

"So is it party time again?" she asks.

I look behind me, wondering if there's someone

else around who she might be talking to. There isn't. "I beg your pardon?"

"Well, it's the weekend. Does that mean you'll be having another party?"

"It wasn't really a party. It was just the people who helped us move."

"Humph! And I suppose you're going to tell me they stayed for coffee. Don't bother even trying that one. I saw the empties your mother was trying to sneak out the next morning."

"I don't think we're expecting any company this weekend."

"Good!" She stubs her cigarette out in a small ceramic pig ashtray and stomps back into her trailer without saying good-bye.

My mom drives me over to Dad's on Saturday morning. She's planning to stay awhile to do some cleaning. When we get to the house, we see the real estate lady's car in the driveway.

"Oh, darn it," says Mom. "She must be showing the place to someone. We probably shouldn't go in."

"Want me to check?" I ask.

"Okay."

I get out of the car and let myself in through the front door. I can hear voices coming from the kitchen. It sounds like it's just Amy and Dad.

"Dad?" I call.

"In here, Lucy," he says.

They're sitting at the table, drinking Starbucks coffee.

"Who bought the coffee?" I ask.

"Me," answers Amy. "Why do you ask?"

"Well, the tall is expensive, but Dad says you can get the same thing from McDonald's or A&W for a whole lot less."

"I prefer Starbucks," says Amy.

"Can Mom come in and clean?" I ask Dad.

"Sure, that will be great."

"Your ex comes in to clean the house?" Amy asks.

"She thinks it will show better if it's kept up right," says Dad. "It's not like I'm leaving my dirty clothes on the floor or anything like that, but Kate notices things I don't. She sort of has an eye for detail."

He's still explaining, but I go to the front door and motion to Mom that it's okay to come in.

Mom has brought the vacuum from our place and she's carrying it as she walks into the kitchen. When she sees Amy and Dad sitting there together, she looks kind of shocked, probably because of the Starbucks coffee.

"I thought you were showing someone through the house," she says.

"Oh no," says Amy. "This is more of a social visit."

"How nice. And will the noise of the vacuum bother you?"

"I told Amy I'll be wanting to buy a smaller house once this place sells," Dad says. "She just dropped by with a few listings she thought I might be interested in."

"I really should be going anyway," Amy says. She stands up and starts toward the door. She's wearing a camel-colored suit with a short slim skirt and really high-heeled shoes. She has very nice legs. She stops for a minute right next to Mom. Mom is wearing blue jeans and a T-shirt with a stretched-out neck. Her hair is in a ponytail. She has no makeup on. Her face is shiny, and the freckles across her nose really show.

Amy looks down at her. "We haven't had an offer yet, but I was telling Harold, a couple has asked to come back for a second look this afternoon. That's always promising."

She wiggles her fingers good-bye at Mom. Then Dad walks her to the door.

Mom drops the vacuum hose and attachment with a thud and stomps off to get a bucket and rag from the laundry room.

"Why don't you and Lucy go out for awhile?" she says when Dad comes back into the kitchen. "I'll be through here in about two hours." She's already scrubbing away at the smeary ceramic top of the stove.

"Well, that doesn't seem right . . ." Dad starts to say.

"Look, I'd rather work alone. Do you mind?"

Dad and I go. We drive down to the beach at White Rock. We hang out there for awhile and do some grocery shopping. By the time we get back, Mom's left. We barely have time to unload our groceries and make ourselves sandwiches before we have to leave again. Amy's bringing those people back to look at the house for a second time. She doesn't like us to be there. She says it works better if the buyers have some privacy. This time, while we're kicked out, we go to look at some of the places Amy's given Dad listings for.

That evening, Dad and I watch *Up in the Air*. It's supposed to be a funny movie – and it is, in a way – but then it takes this twist and the ending is kind of sad. I don't think it cheers Dad up much. It's over about ten-thirty and we both head upstairs to bed at the same time. I get into my pj's and am in the bathroom, brushing my teeth, when I hear Dad.

"What the heck? Gross!" He's in the en suite bathroom. He's been brushing his teeth too. Now he's rinsing his mouth out with water. He spits into the sink and holds his toothbrush out for me to see. It looks normal. "Have you been using this toothbrush to clean things?"

"Of course not. I never clean anything."

"It tastes like that cleanser stuff."

"Sometimes Mom uses an old toothbrush to clean around the taps or to do the hinges on the toilet seat lid."

"Yuck!" he screams. He grabs the mouthwash and chugs it straight from the bottle. "But it was in the holder where I always keep it. It's in perfectly good shape. There's no way she could have thought . . ."

"Well, maybe it fell in the toilet or something, so she thought she might as well use it to clean."

"Is that supposed to make me feel better?"

"Well, no, but you were wondering."

"And if it fell in the toilet and she used it to clean around the hinges of the seat, why would she put it back in the holder where I always keep it?"

I shrug.

"A person would have to be crazy to do something like that," he says.

"Or mad." Mom's not crazy, but it's pretty easy to imagine her being mad.

"She seemed funny from the minute she walked in today. Did she say anything? Why would she be mad at me?"

"Maybe about the coffee," I answer.

"What do you mean, 'about the coffee'? She didn't even have any coffee."

"But you and Amy were drinking Starbucks."

"So?"

"Well, you said so yourself, it's more expensive."

"I didn't buy it. Amy brought it with her."

"I know, but did you tell Amy that she should have bought it at McDonald's?"

"No, I guess not," he says. "Do you think she's jealous?"

"Amy?"

"No, your mom."

"I don't know. I think if she's mad, it's probably about the coffee."

"I bet she's jealous." He's starting to smile. I can tell he likes the idea.

He searches in the back of one of the vanity drawers and finds a new toothbrush that's still in its packaging.

I leave him brushing his teeth. He's in a much better mood.

When Dad drops me off at home on Sunday night, Mom is sitting at the kitchen table, doing the crossword puzzle. She's nowhere near finished, but when I come in, she pushes it to one side. I pick it up and have a look. I don't really expect to be able to help. She and Dad are the ones who like doing these things.

"Five across is *adagio*," I say. The clue says, "Slow time in music."

She looks surprised. She checks the puzzle. It fits. "Since when did you know about music?" she asks.

"I only know that because Dad was doing the same puzzle at his house. He had me look the answer up on the Internet."

They always used to do *The New York Times* crossword together on Sundays.

Mom fills in the word and puts the puzzle away half-done. Dad didn't finish it either.

I tell Mom about the houses we saw. They were older than our house, and the neighborhoods weren't so upscale, but some were nice enough. Sort of like the street Siobhan lives on. "When our house sells and you're looking for another place to buy, maybe we could drive around Siobhan's subdivision," I tell Mom. I figure, if we are going to be a bit poor, it would be nice if I lived near Siobhan and we could be poor together.

"I'm not sure that I'm going to be buying another house right away," Mom says.

"Why not?" I ask. "Like you said yourself, this place is kind of depressing."

"Well, it's not my dream home, but it will do for awhile."

"But once you get your share of the money from the house, why would you want to stay here?"

"I might go back to school. If I do that, it will mean quitting my job."

I just about fall off my chair. "But why?" I ask. "You already have your grade twelve. You even took those extra bookkeeping courses. You have the perfect job!"

"Do you know that I've worked at that convent for almost half my life?"

She's exaggerating. It can't be any more than ten years. And the way she always calls it "the convent" makes it sound like it's just her and a bunch of nuns. It's not that way at all. The sisters at Cenacle Heights run a retreat center. They have workshops and days of reflection. Lots of church groups meet there. They even have school classes visit sometimes, like mine did when we were getting ready for confirmation.

Grandma and Sister Margaret Mary are friends, so sometimes we just go up there for tea. It's a really nice place: quiet and holy. The gardens are very peaceful. And it's not like Mom is making up beds and washing toilets anymore. That was her first job there, but after she and Dad got married, she took some bookkeeping courses, so now she works in the office. Most people would kill for a job like hers.

"Does Grandma know about this idea of yours?"

"I'm not telling her till I know for sure that I'm going," she says. "I might not even get in."

"Get in where?" I cannot see my mother going to university. What kind of a job would she get when she graduated? I can just imagine someone with her temper being a teacher or a nurse.

"I've applied to BCIT," she says.

That's the B.C. Institute of Technology. I think they offer computer courses there. She's never shown much interest in the computer. It's Dad and I who hog it most of the time.

"I've applied for their course in interior design."

"To be like an interior decorator?"

She nods.

"You don't need to take a course. You know how to do that already."

"But if I could take that course, I'd end up with the credentials that I need to do that for a job. I'd be a professional."

"Like the ones you see on the decorating channel?"

"Yeah, sort of like them."

It doesn't seem like such a bad idea. "You'd be good at that."

She gives a happy smile like I've said something

wonderful. "I'm so glad you think so. I haven't told anyone because I thought you'd all laugh at me."

"Who did you think would laugh?"

"Well, not laugh exactly, but think I was stupid and try to talk me out of it."

"Who'd do that?"

"I thought you would, and Grandma and your dad."

"You never even told Dad?"

"No. Can't you just imagine the state it would send him into? It would totally destroy his precious budget."

"He's good at budgets," I say. "Maybe he could have done a new one."

She just shrugs.

What I don't understand is, what all this has to do with us having to stay here. I know right now it's all we can afford, but I was counting on moving back to Surrey once our big house sold. I can't stand this place much longer. The trailer I'm getting used to; it's the school scene that sucks. The work is easy and there are a couple of teachers I really like, but I always have Brandy, that weird girl with the blue and black hair, "accidentally" bumping me or making snotty comments. Harbie and Kuldeep are nice, but we aren't really friends. It's more like they're just being polite.

"But we'll be getting thousands of dollars when the house sale goes through. Going to school won't cost that much, will it?" I ask.

"It's not cheap. The fees are about four thousand dollars a year, but the big thing is that I'll have to quit my job. I won't be able to get a mortgage if I'm not working."

"How long is the course?"

"Two years. Can't you just see your dad going for that? He'd want me to wait till you finished college."

Waiting doesn't seem like such a bad idea. Better for me than trying to stay clear of Brandy for two years. In the meantime, we could buy a new house and Mom could practice being an interior decorator by designing another really sensational bedroom for me. If we got one of those older houses, she could do up the rec room in the basement so I'd have someplace super fancy to entertain Siobhan and my other friends, if I had any. I might even get to be popular. I don't tell her what I'm thinking. Like she says, maybe she won't even get in to BCIT.

eleven

I phone Siobhan after school on Monday, but she can't talk for long. Her mother wants her to help one of her brothers, so she has to hang up. I wonder how we're going to stay friends if I never get to see her. Mom doesn't have problems like that. Gina's got nothing better to do than drive miles to drop in for a coffee. Mom and I are just finishing up the dinner dishes when we hear a car pull up next to the trailer. Mom looks out the window to see who it is.

"Hey, it's Gina." She dries her hands and heads for the door.

"Shouldn't you be at pilates?" I ask as soon as Gina steps inside.

It's six-thirty and she and Mom always went to a seven o'clock class on Mondays and Fridays.

"I'm playing hooky. It's just not the same without you," she says, talking to my mom, not me. She plops herself down at the table, sitting on one chair and putting her feet up on another. "You got anything to drink?"

"Just cola," says Mom.

Gina shrugs. "Guess that'll do."

Mom was figuring out our budget this morning, and she's left the paper she was scribbling on, along with a couple of bills, in a slot of the napkin holder, which is sitting in the center of the table. While Mom's getting the colas and putting ice into the glasses, nosy Gina helps herself to a look at our finances.

"What's this?" she asks.

"Just a list to show what I've spent this month," Mom says.

"Hmm, movie rentals $7.00, stamps $5.45. This is so sad! Well, at least you're not writing down what you pay for every cup of coffee."

"That's because I haven't been able to afford to go out for coffee."

"It can't be that bad. Why are you fussing so much about it? I thought Harold was the one who was totally anal about money. When did *you* start writing down everything you spend?"

Mom looks embarrassed. She skids a pop across the table to Gina. "I guess as soon as Harold wasn't here to do it."

Since no one's paying any attention to either me or the dog, we go to my room. I leave the door open so I can still hear Gina and Mom talking.

"So how long has it been? Three weeks, right?"

"Since I moved in here? Yeah, three weeks this Sunday."

"Okay already, then that's quite enough of the hermit act. It's time you got out and about."

"Oh, I don't know. I'm so broke, and there's Lucy to think of."

"She'll be with Harold on the weekend anyway. Ian and I've been talking. We're taking you clubbing. Our treat."

"I couldn't . . ."

They talk for a good half hour. Mom keeps making excuses, but Gina is very pushy. She just won't take no for an answer. By the time she leaves, Mom has agreed that Ian and Gina can pick her up at nine on Friday night. What time is that to be going out? It's almost bedtime!

I'm so upset, I'm almost speechless. As soon as Gina leaves, I confront Mom. "You're going to a nightclub?"

"So it seems."

"That's disgusting. I suppose you'll wear an indecent dress like that one Gina was wearing in the picture she showed us that time."

"Don't I wish! I'll just wear jeans and my lime floral top. It's all I have."

I can imagine what Grandma and Dad will have to say about this. I head for the phone.

"Lucy!"

She doesn't actually yell, but she says it so sharply I stop like I've been slapped.

"Don't even think about it."

I leave the phone alone and stomp back to my bedroom. The dog is sleeping on my bed. She could use a walk. I wake her up, go get her leash, and we walk out the door without even looking back at Mom.

Maybe Mom can make me too uncomfortable to use the phone in front of her, but she can't stop me from talking to Dad when she drops me off at his place on Friday. He's managed to get home at a decent time, but there's nothing to eat in the house, so we have to go grocery shopping before we can make dinner.

We're driving to the store, but my mind is a thousand miles away.

"You're awfully quiet tonight," he says. "Is something bothering you?"

"It's that Gina again. She and Ian are taking Mom out to a nightclub."

"She's going to a nightclub? She never told me she'd like to go to a nightclub. Did she ever mention it to you?"

"No, and it wasn't her who suggested it on Monday either. It's all Gina's idea. Mom even argued about it at first, but you know what it's like. Gina seems to be able to brainwash her."

The traffic is heavy, like it always is on Friday nights. Dad changes lanes.

"By the time Gina left, all Mom was worrying about was that she didn't have a really sexy dress to wear."

"No, I guess she wouldn't."

"She's going to wear jeans and her new lime top."

I imagine he'll feel better knowing this. At least she'll be dressed decently. He knows which top it is; she doesn't have a lot of clothes.

"She looks cute in that," he says.

"But do most people go clubbing in ordinary clothes like that?"

"I wouldn't know."

"You've never been?"

"No." He pulls the van into the Save-On-Foods parking lot. Once he's parked, we get out and he pulls out one of the carts from the stand. He wheels it toward the store.

"When you and Mom were dating, what sorts of things did you do?" I ask.

"We went out for dinner or to a movie sometimes."

The way he says that, it doesn't sound like they did that very often. "What else did you do?"

"Other times, we'd just stay home and play cards with your grandma and granddad. On the weekends, we'd take you to the park."

It doesn't sound that romantic. We're in the pasta and sauce aisle. Dad's pitching boxes of Kraft Dinner into the shopping cart while he's talking.

"Dad!"

"What?"

I can't believe he hasn't noticed. "Look, the store brand is four cents less a box."

"So it is."

He starts putting the Kraft Dinner back on the shelf.
I gather up half a dozen boxes of the store brand macaroni dinner and put them in the cart. This breakup is
really affecting him. I wonder if he's losing it. He's
probably worried too, because he says we need to con-
centrate more on the shopping.

We're in the car driving home when he picks up the
conversation we were having before.

"We went to a lot of garage sales. Some people
would think that was dull, but your mom always liked
doing that, and I sort of got in to it. I was living in this
dingy bachelor pad, and she was determined to make it
into a real home."

I nod. That sounds like Mom.

"She did too, with bits and pieces we picked up for
almost nothing." He's smiling a bit as he says this, but
by the time we get home, he looks sad again.

He must be brooding about it, because it's got to be
an hour later when, out of the blue, he says, "No
wonder she left me."

"It's not your fault."

"Probably not. It's just who I am. That's the worst
of it. It's not something I can change."

I don't know what he's talking about. There's
nothing wrong with who he is. He's not movie-star
handsome, but he's nice-looking enough. He's quite tall
and he's not fat. He has short brown hair and eyes that
squint at the corners in a friendly way when he smiles.

He only wears his glasses when he's working or when he's tired.

"I think you're very nice looking," I say.

"Thanks, but that's not what I'm talking about. I'm so dull and boring. I'm just not a fun kind of person."

I sort of know what he means. I'm not a fun person either. Everyone says I'm too serious. Sometimes the kids at school give me a hard time about the way I talk. They say I sound like a teacher or something.

"I think part of it is being an only child. Both your mom and I had older parents too. That's why I thought we were well-suited to each other."

"Just because you both had old parents?"

"No, because we were both weird only children with no social skills."

I don't like him talking like this. It makes me very uncomfortable, probably because I bet some people would say that I'm a weird only child with no social skills too.

It's time to change the subject.

"You know," I say, "You could just be feeling down because you need to eat. Look how late it is. Grandma says low blood sugar can really affect your mood."

I get the loaf of bread out, put six slices on the cutting board, and start buttering them. "Will ham and cheese be okay?"

"Sounds good," he says.

*

When Dad drops me off at the trailer on Sunday evening, the dog is just crazy-excited to see me. She is jumping all over me and doing those doggy bows that mean she wants to play. She puts her butt up in the air and her chest on the floor, and unless you make a fuss over her right away, she barks.

Mom is lying on the couch, reading a book. She laughs at the dog. "Take her out for awhile, Lucy. She'll like that and it will calm her down."

That's true. I toss my backpack on the chair and pick up her leash from the corner of the counter. I don't forget the plastic bags.

When we get back, the dog is much calmer. Mom is still lying there, reading. It's a fat library book, and she's almost finished it.

"So how was the nightclubbing?" I ask.

"Noisy."

"Did you have a good time?"

"Well, I guess it was educational."

What kind of an answer is that? What did she learn? Do I really want to know? "Did you dance?"

"A bit. Mostly we just sat around and talked, which was pretty weird."

"Why's it weird to sit around and talk?" That sounds to me like a civilized way to spend an evening. Why go out with your friends if you aren't even going to talk to them?

"It was weird because we couldn't hear each other. I spent all evening yelling over the music. My throat was so sore I could barely talk when I got home."

"Who did you dance with?"

"You don't really have to dance with a particular person. People just dance in a group sometimes."

"So you'd dance with Ian and Gina, the three of you being a group?"

"We met Jake there too."

Who's Jake? I don't remember her talking about anyone named Jake. She must notice that I'm puzzled.

"Jake. You remember Jake. The guy who lives down the way here. He helped us the day we moved in."

How could I forget? He's the one I thought might be hot if he cleaned himself up a bit. "Did he get cleaned up to go to the nightclub?"

Mom looks at me like I've lost it. "Of course he was cleaned up. Did you think he'd crawl out from under the hood of his car and head out to a nightclub just as he was?"

I don't answer. So he probably looked hot.

"So what did you do yesterday?" I ask.

"Mostly just read this book," she says. "There isn't much housework to do around here, is there? It's not like having a big house."

"How many drinks did you have at the club?"

"A couple."

"That's what everyone says."

"What's that supposed to mean?"

"Well, maybe there's a reason you've spent the whole weekend lying on the couch."

She's sitting up now, glaring at me.

"You sure you don't have a hangover?"

"Lucy, go to your room. Right now, before I do or say something we'll both regret."

She says this without even raising her voice, which is not like her. Still, she sounds like she means it. I go to my room, but now I'm really worried. When I accused her of having a hangover, I didn't really think she had one. I just wondered about it because, even if I am a weird only child with no social skills, I know that most people do not go to nightclubs and drink coffee. The way she reacted, though, makes me sure I hit a sore spot. Siobhan and I were reading some brochures Mariah brought us from her Alateen group last week. Most alcoholics feel guilty about their drinking and are really in to denial.

twelve

On Monday, I'm on the phone with Grandma when Mom gets home. I say good-bye and hang up just as she comes in the door. Mom heads down the hall to her room to change. She's still in her room when I hear a funny sound, like someone is bumping up against the side of our trailer. The dog starts to bark. I look outside but don't see anyone right away. The dog is still barking; she wants out. I open the door and follow her outside. She heads for the lean-to at the side of the trailer, and just then, our landlord, that Randy, comes around the corner.

"Why are you hanging around our shed?" I ask.

He looks surprised to see me, but still he acts friendly. "You're Kate's daughter, right?"

"Right," I say. "What are you doing out here?"

"You're Lucy, right?"

"Right. What were you doing behind our shed?"

He laughs. "It's my shed. I have an agreement with your mom. She gets the trailer, but I get to keep my stuff in the shed."

I remember the first time Mom showed me the trailer. I wondered then if there would be a door to the lean-to from the inside of our house. There isn't. I haven't thought anything more about it. "How do you get in there?" I ask.

"Door's on the other end there," he says, pointing. "But don't even try. That's one big lock I have on it. I don't want anyone ripping me off. It's a problem when the whole world knows you're in camp for weeks at a time."

"It seems kind of early for camping," I say.

He looks puzzled, but then he smiles at me. "I'm not camping, I'm logging with an outfit up in the Queen Charlottes. We fly in there and stay in camp for ten days, then I'm home for five."

"So where do you live when you're not in camp?"

"With Jake," he says, and he points down the road to Jake's trailer.

The dog has quit barking and is now standing beside Randy. Randy bends over and gives her a pat. Then he walks away. I watch him go off and I go back inside.

As soon as Mom comes out of her bedroom to start making dinner, I ask, "Did you hear the dog barking while you were getting changed?"

"I'd have to be deaf not to. What set her off?"

"It was that Randy. He was in the shed. He says he's allowed to go in there whenever he wants."

"Yeah, he's storing some of his things there. Did he say if Jake was home?"

"No, he didn't say anything about Jake. Have you seen what he has in there?"

"Where?"

"In the shed."

"No, who cares what he has in the shed? Did he say when he got back?"

Sometimes I wonder if my mom suffers from attention deficit disorder. She can never seem to keep her mind on the subject. "It could be something illegal," I say. "Anyway, it makes me nervous, him just sneaking around here like that. What if I'd been alone?"

"I'll ask him not to come without calling first." She slides the casserole she made this morning into the oven.

"I'll go over right now. I want to talk to Jake anyway," she says.

She's out the door before I can ask her what Jake has to do with it. I'm tempted to follow her, but instead, I watch from the front window. I can see Jake's place from there. She knocks on the door, but she doesn't go in. I can't see who answers. She talks a minute and then comes back.

"Why did you want to talk to Jake?" I ask.

"Nothing important. He wasn't home anyway. He's on a run to California."

"What's he doing there?"

"Delivering stuff, I guess. He drives a truck for a living. I told Randy he scared you and he shouldn't come round without calling me first."

This is just so not the point! "Don't you wonder at all what he's got in that shed?"

"No, I don't wonder at all. It's none of my business. Or yours. I have more important things to worry about. Now set the table."

You really can't talk to her when she gets in one of these moods, so I give it up for the time being.

After dinner, I sit down at the table to do my English homework and Mom settles down with her book. I'm doing this exercise where we pick out the subject, the verb, and the object in each sentence. It's easy. I'm good at English. I'm almost finished all the questions when I hit this weird one. The sentence reads, "Most of all, Susan hated jogging."

I write "Subject – Susan, Verb – hated, Object – jogging."

Then I look at it again. The subject and the object are always nouns. Jogging is a verb. Who did the action? Susan. What did she do? Hated. What did she hate? Jogging. Jogging has got to be the object, but it's not a noun.

"Mom, will you look at this?" I show her the sentence and explain why I'm confused.

"This is a bit much for grade eight," she says. "I wonder where your teacher got this worksheet."

"Why does it matter?"

"Well the word *jogging* is a gerund. I don't think I took gerunds till I was in grade eleven or twelve."

She explains that I'm not going crazy and that "jogging" is the object but it is also a verb. She says gerunds are verbs that end in *ing* and are used like nouns. She gives me a bunch of examples. Anyone hearing us talk about my homework would think it was a really dull conversation. They'd never guess how much excitement it was going to cause in my life.

It's two days later, in English class, that this stupid gerund gets me into a mess of trouble. Or maybe the real problem is that I never know when to keep my mouth shut. Ms. Phillips has marked our homework assignments and is handing them back. I have every answer right except one. I had said that *jogging* was the object of the sentence. There's a red *X* by that answer.

I put my hand up and ask, "Why did you mark this one wrong?"

"It's a verb," she answers.

"No, it's not," I reply. "It's a gerund."

"What do you know about gerunds?"

I tell her. She looks at the sentence again and agrees that I'm right. She explains it to the class. She tells everyone how brilliant I am, how this is grade twelve material, and how she'd overlooked it herself. She says I must be really advanced.

From behind my left ear, I hear these sucking noises.

"Brandy," says Ms. Phillips. "It's rude to whisper to Lucy when I'm speaking."

"Sorry."

We go on with our work.

Brandy jabs me in the back with her ballpoint pen.

"Oops," she says. "Sorry."

I'm glad when class is over so I can get away from her, but I don't get much of a break.

I'm sitting with Harbie at lunch when Brandy and her two friends come up.

"This is the motormouth." She sneers down at me. "Teacher's little pet." She turns to her friends, "You wouldn't believe this kid. She's such a dweeb." She puts on this silly high-pitched voice, "Oh, Ms. Phillips, this is so exciting. Is it a noun or is it a verb . . . blah, blah, blah!"

She's standing so close to me that I have to lean back in my seat or her boobs would be touching my face. The more she talks, the madder she sounds. It's like she's working herself into a rage. She gives my shoulder a shove.

"Hey guys, what's happening?"

I look past Brandy. A boy's come up and is standing by Brandy's two friends. He's smiling. He's obviously not in touch with the situation.

"No problem, is there?" he asks.

Brandy looks at him and shrugs. "No, I guess not. I'm just venting."

He nods. "Well, sometimes you need to do that. Anyway, see you around."

Then he sits down next to me with his tray of food. Brandy and her friends walk away and go to another table.

"Thanks," says Harbie, who's been sitting there speechless all through the rant.

I look at her and then look back at the boy. I'm

confused. He looks familiar. Harbie seems to know him, but I'm sure he isn't one of the people she's introduced me to.

"This is my brother," she says. "Rob, this is Lucy. She's new."

He looks straight at me for the first time. "Have we met before? You look familiar."

I look back at him. I feel my cheeks getting warm. I look down at my half-eaten container of yogurt. "Yeah," I say. "I'm the dog poop girl."

He's just taken a drink from a can of pop, but when he hears my reply, he sprays ginger ale out of his nose and starts laughing.

Harbie looks confused. Rob still can't talk, so I tell her. "I was walking a dog and she pooped in your yard. Your brother made me clean it up."

By now, Rob can talk again. "That was our grandparents' place."

That makes sense. They wouldn't be going to school here if they lived in Surrey. He asks if I moved. I tell him I did, but that when I was up by his grandma's place, I was just visiting. He's actually quite nice, also rather good-looking.

I wish I had an older brother. He could walk me home from school and provide protection. What will happen if I'm alone and I meet up with Brandy someplace? It's bound to happen sooner or later. How am I supposed to avoid someone who lives almost next door to me and goes to the same school as I do?

For starters, I decide I have to find a different way to get home. That afternoon, instead of walking toward our trailer park, I go down the street in the opposite direction. Then I cut over a few blocks and walk back, so in the end I've gone in sort of a circle. It takes me almost an hour.

I'm dragging myself up the steps to our door, thinking how good it will feel to get a snack and just veg out for a bit, when I hear the dog start to bark. How could I forget the dog? I'm going to have to take her out. I've walked over a mile out of my way to avoid Brandy, and now I'll probably bump into her anyway. I look at the dog. Why couldn't she be a German shepherd or a pit bull?

We do the world's shortest walk. We don't meet Brandy.

thirteen

As if I don't have enough stress in my life, we're barely finished the dinner dishes when Gina arrives. Has she never heard of the phone? Does she always just have to show up uninvited? She probably wants Mom to go out drinking again this weekend. The dog starts to bark at her. Good for the dog!

"I just made tea." Mom takes two mugs from the cupboard and goes over and sits down with Gina at the table.

I'm standing there with a dish towel in my hands. There's nothing left to dry.

"You can finish up there, Lucy. There's just the pots left."

Just the pots? We had barbecued ribs! The sauce has baked onto the rack and the pan that goes under it. It will take me all night. I can't believe this. We are probably the only people in Langley without a dishwasher.

At first I'm banging pots and pans around and not paying any attention to what Mom and Gina are talking about. But then I hear Jake's name.

"So where are you two going?" Gina asks.

"We're not going anywhere. I told you, I never said I'd go out with him."

"Well, that's not what he told Ian."

"When did Ian talk to him?"

"That night, while you and I were in the washroom."

"I don't know how he got that idea. I went over there yesterday, thinking I could straighten it out, but he's on a run to California. Randy says he won't be back till a week Friday."

"That's the night he's expecting you to go out with him. You can't just meet him on the doorstep and tell him it was all a mistake."

"Why not?" I ask.

"Butt out, Lucy," Gina says. Then she turns her attention back to Mom. I look at Mom too. She's glaring at Gina like she's about to give her a piece of her mind. Then she glances over at me. I just give a shrug. Gina's always rude. I'm not about to take it personally. Mom goes back to picking at the pattern on her mug like she expects bits of the glaze to flake off.

Gina has skin as thick as a rhinoceros; she hasn't noticed a thing. "But you like him, don't you?"

"He seems nice enough."

"Come on. I think it's a bit more than that," Gina says. "You couldn't take your eyes off him all night."

"Well, he kept talking."

"So? What's that got to do with it?"

"I couldn't hear him over the noise. I'd catch bits, but a lot of the time, I was trying to fill in the blank parts by lipreading."

"But you just kept smiling and nodding. He thinks you're crazy about him."

Mom blushes. So she should.

"Has anyone bothered to tell Jake that you're married?" I ask.

They both look at me.

"He knows she's separated," Gina replies.

"She's still married, even if she and Dad aren't living together. She'll always be married to him in God's eyes."

Gina scowls at me. "Look, Pope Lucy, your mom's only twenty-eight years old. You can't expect her to live the life of a nun."

"Well, I don't expect her to behave like a slut either."

"What a mouth you've got on you. If you were mine, I'd smack you one. Maybe you should worry about your own sins for a change."

Mom's sitting motionless, holding her head in both hands. Then she gets up like she hasn't heard anything and picks up the dog's leash. "Come on, Lucy. Let's go for a walk."

The dog never needs to be asked twice. She scrambles up from her place on the couch, and she and Mom walk out and leave Gina and me alone in the trailer, looking at each other. We might have started arguing again, but just then the phone rings. I answer it. It's my dad. I'd have thought things couldn't get any worse, but they do. When I tell him Mom is out walking the dog, he asks me to give her a message.

"We have an offer on the house. Amy's bringing it by at six tomorrow. Can you have your mom give me a call?"

"Sure."

What more is there to say? Why is it such a shock? I knew the house was up for sale. Someone was bound to buy it sooner or later. Still, it isn't until this minute that it all seems real to me.

"Excuse me," I say to Gina when I hang up. I go to my room. I don't feel like talking anymore.

When Mom comes back, I stick my head out and say, "Dad called."

"For you or for me?"

"For you. Someone's made an offer on the house. Amy wants to bring it by tomorrow. You're supposed to call him."

Mom sits down hard.

"Wow! That's great news," says Gina.

"I guess."

Gina frowns. "What to you mean, you guess? You want to sell the place, right?"

"Right."

"So an offer is good news, right?"

"I suppose so . . . it seems so final."

"I thought you wanted final. I thought you wanted to make a life of your own."

"I do. I do."

"You can quit your job. You can take your course. You can buy another house on your own. You won't have to listen to Harold fussing about finances 24-7."

"No," Mom mutters. "I'll be the one fussing about the money."

"Well, don't do it in front of Jake or any other boyfriend you might have. It will completely turn them off."

Turned off is how I feel. I don't want to hear any more of this conversation. I just want to be by myself. This place is so small, that even though I've shut myself up in my room, I can still hear almost everything they say. I come out of my room and grab the leash.

"Come on. Let's go for a walk."

"I just walked her," Mom says.

"She wants to go out again. Look at her."

The dog is dancing around, all keen and excited. Maybe she's got a short memory and has forgotten that she just got back from a walk about two minutes ago. I snap her leash on. I'm not afraid to walk her now. If I accidentally pass by Brandy's place, it won't matter because it's dark enough that she won't know it's me.

We walk a long time. It seems funny that Gina's the only one who hasn't taken the dog for a walk tonight. Some pet owner *she* is.

The next morning, I ask Mom if she'll drive me to school.

She looks up from the coffee cup she's been staring into. "Why? If I drop you off on my way to work, you'll get there just after eight. That's way too early."

"I don't care. There are worse things."

"Do you have a lot of stuff to carry again?"

"No."

"Why don't you walk?" She glances out the window. "It's not like it's raining."

"Remember how I told you about Harbie and Kuldeep?"

She nods.

"They're not the only girls I met."

I tell her about Brandy. She says she'll give me a ride this morning, but tonight she wants us to find out where Brandy lives so she can go talk to her mother.

"You can't do that! Brandy will kill me if she finds out I squealed."

"Well, I'm not going to have you afraid to leave the house because of Brandy's bullying. Her mother has got to accept some responsibility."

"I told you about her skirt."

"You said it barely covered her bottom."

"And about her hair?"

"I heard you, black with royal blue streaks."

"So does that sound like she listens to her mother?"

Mom dumps the last of her coffee down the sink. "We'll talk about it tonight. We need a better plan. You're not going to be able to avoid her forever."

She's right.

At lunchtime, when Harbie and I get to the cafeteria, Rob is sitting at a table with his friend Trevor. They haven't got any food yet, so they stand up and we all go to the serving tables together. I get a bowl of chili and a cup of chocolate milk. I'm carrying them on a tray and following Rob back to the table. Harbie's behind me.

We have to pass the table where Brandy's sitting. I'm right next to it when I trip over something. I stumble forward and my tray hits Rob in the back. He spins around and grabs my shoulder with one free hand so I don't fall. He drops his tray in the process. I hang on to mine, but the bowl of chili has crashed onto the floor and the whole tray is awash in spilled chocolate milk. It's all down the front of my skirt and T-shirt. Rob has chili on his back. Brandy and her friends are laughing.

"Jennifer, say you're sorry. I mean, it's not your fault your size 10 feet were sticking out, but look what you've done," gloats Brandy.

The girl she's talking to says "Sorry."

Then they all laugh some more. I don't even bother looking at them. I'm looking at Rob. He's got splatters of pop on the front of his shirt. He's still hanging on to my shoulder. He's very close.

"Are you okay?" he asks.

I nod. "But look what I've done. I've spilled my chili on your back and when you grabbed me, your pop splashed all over."

He looks down at himself. "Don't worry about it. I can change in to the T-shirt I use for gym."

I think then he notices that he's still hanging on to me because he lets go. We both bend down and start trying to clean up the mess. Someone must have called the custodian, because while we're still trying to scoop up chili with napkins, he comes along with a mop and dustpan.

Rob's lost his drink, but his hamburger is okay. I have no lunch at all now, and I don't have money to buy something else. Like I'd want to anyway. I've got chocolate milk all down the front of me. Who wants to sit around like that?

"I'm going home to change."

Harbie looks at my clothes. "Yeah, you need to rinse out your skirt or it will stain."

I hadn't thought of that. I just want to get out of here. I try to walk tall and look dignified as I leave the cafeteria. It's not easy, being so short and now with food slopped all down the front of me, but I do the best I can.

I drop by the office to tell the secretary that I'm leaving, and then I head for home. The good part is that I don't have to take some weird circular route this time. Brandy's still back at school, eating her lunch and laughing with her friends.

The dog is glad to see me and starts barking because she expects a walk. I pick her up, and she's distracted right away because I smell so interesting. She starts sniffing and licking my shirt. I feel sticky all over, so I strip off my clothes, throw them on the bathroom floor, and step into the shower.

When I'm finished my shower, I put on my grungy

bathrobe and go out to the kitchen to make myself a cheese sandwich. I give the dog little tastes. It's past one o'clock. I told the secretary I was going home to change. So I'll change. I didn't say I'd come back. I decide I'm not going to.

I clean up my dishes and hang my dirty, wet clothes on the shower rod. Then I go look for something clean to wear. I put on a pair of jeans. I'm thinking about Rob standing so close to me like that. I wish I could be at least a bit hot. It's not fair that some girls get all the boobs.

I wander into Mom's room and start looking in her drawers. She's got this one really fancy bra. It's lace and it's got push-up pads and underwire. I try it on. It fits around my chest pretty well, but there's not much of me to fill the cups. I go into my own room and get a pair of socks. I stuff one in each side of the bra. It takes a bit of adjusting, but it looks pretty good. I don't have any cleavage, but if I put a T-shirt on, I bet the boobs would look real. I pull on a T-shirt. It fits tightly now. I can make out the pattern of the lace through the material. It looks sexy but not too obvious.

Things would have been different when Rob found himself holding on to me if I'd looked like this. I start poking through Mom's makeup. I put on some foundation. Then I try eyeliner and mascara, copying the way I'd seen Mom do it. I stand back to admire the effect. I let my eyelids droop like the models do. Not that I'd look this way at just anyone, only at my husband or maybe my fiancé. I put on lipstick. I have trouble making it even, but if I don't look too close, it's okay. I stand back from the mirror to get the whole picture. I pose with my chest out to make the most of my boobs. I pout my mouth and try to look sexy. I imagine what it would be like if I were getting dressed up like this to go out on a date with Rob. He would definitely think I was a hottie.

Grandma wouldn't approve at all, but there really wouldn't be anything for her to worry about. I'd never be tempted to go too far. There's no way I'd ever get naked with a guy when my boobs are a pair of gym socks. I'll probably stay a virgin forever – and it won't be because I made a promise to God.

I wash the makeup off and put Mom's bra and my socks back where they belong. Brandy won't be home for another hour, so I take the dog for a proper walk while it's safe to do it. I see Mrs. Warren, the lady from the pig house, eyeing me through her front window. When I get back, I call Grandma. It's Granddad who answers the phone. Grandma isn't home. She's out playing bridge. This is so weird. Grandma never goes out.

fourteen

Mom gets home a little after five. She's getting out of her car when Mrs. Warren comes out of her trailer and starts talking to her. I watch them from the window. I can't hear what they're saying.

"So I hear you played hooky this afternoon," Mom says as soon as she comes in the door.

"I had to come home to clean up because I had food all over my clothes. Brandy's friend tripped me when I was carrying my lunch tray."

She scowls. "Maybe I should talk to the principal on Monday."

"Do you want to get me killed? Brandy will just get me someplace away from the school. The principal can't do anything about that."

I wish I could think of something to do about it myself, but I can't. I guess I just have to hang around waiting for Brandy to find the right time and place to pounce on me.

I reach for a tissue.

Mom puts her arm around me. "We'll think of something."

I just stand there, snuffling on her shoulder for a bit.

"Why don't you call Siobhan?" she suggests. "Maybe you could visit her this evening since tomorrow is Saturday. That would make you feel better."

That's so true. Being around Siobhan might ease the sadness. I think of the cake she brought to school. She really likes me. I'm scared that Brandy might get physical, but even if someone could give me a guarantee that she wouldn't, I'd still feel awful just because she hates me so much. Knowing someone likes me a lot really would make me feel better.

"Maybe she could stay over," I say.

"There's not much room here."

"Maybe we could stay at Dad's. You have to go there to sign those papers anyway. You could drop me off tonight instead of tomorrow morning."

Mom nods. "That would work. You better check with your dad."

I call him. He says there's no problem.

I call Siobhan's house. They're eating dinner, and her mom sounds mad when she answers the phone.

That's okay, though, because Siobhan sounds happy to talk to me, and when I ask if she can come spend the night with me at Dad's house, her mom says yes.

Mom and I finish dinner at about six-thirty, so we're kind of rushed. I haven't walked the dog since two in the afternoon. I don't know when Mom will be home to walk her again.

"Maybe we should take the dog," I say. "Siobhan and I could take her for a walk at our other house. No one wants to kill me there."

Mom has gathered up her keys and is halfway out the door. "Bring her along then. You might even want to keep her overnight."

I hadn't thought of that. "Don't you want to keep her?" I ask.

"You've spoiled her, letting her sleep on your bed. She expects to sleep with me when you aren't home."

"So?"

"I don't know how you stand the doggie nightmares. She's always yipping and scrabbling with her feet. I wake up every time."

I don't. I've heard her bark and seen her do running motions with her legs when she's having a daytime nap, but I didn't know she did these things at night. I lift her into the car. It will be nice to have her at Dad's. I sleep better with company.

We pick Siobhan up and then drive over to the house. Amy's car is in the driveway. Before getting out of the car, Mom flips down the visor and checks her face in the mirror. Then she gets out, straightens her skirt, and adjusts the shoulder strap of her bag. Finally she marches toward the house. Siobhan and I follow after her.

We ring the bell and Dad yells, "Come in!"

He and Amy are sitting at the kitchen table. I wonder how long Amy's been here. Maybe Mom's wondering too.

"I'm not late, am I?" she asks.

The clock on the stove says it's 6:55, so she knows darn well she's early.

"No," says Amy. "Come sit down, Kate. Now that you're here, we can get down to business."

So if it's time to get down to business now, what were she and Dad doing before? Mom sits down with them at the table. I go to the fridge to see if there are any snacks. There are some green seedless grapes. I wash them and use a pair of scissors to snip them into small bunches. I can only make the chore take so long. Finally, I go into the family room, where Siobhan is waiting for me. I hand her the grapes and turn on the TV, but I keep the volume really low. I gesture toward the kitchen so Siobhan understands that I'm trying to hear what Mom, Dad, and Amy are saying.

Dad says the offer isn't bad but that probably the people who made it would pay a bit more if they had to. Amy agrees it's worth a try. After some more discussion, Amy makes some changes on the papers and Mom and Dad sign them.

"That's a reasonable counteroffer," Amy says. "I think they'll go for that."

I head back to the fridge and get a couple of cans of pop. Siobhan follows me.

Amy doesn't seem to be in any hurry to leave. She

takes her time packing up her papers. Then she starts asking Dad if he plays golf. He doesn't. She says he should really try it.

Mom's hardly said a word since we got here. She picks up a library book that Dad's left on the table. She pulls out the crossword puzzle he's used as a bookmark and lays the book facedown so she doesn't lose his page. She takes a pencil from her bag and fills in a couple of words. Then she puts the puzzle back where it was and pushes the book to one side.

"Have you read much of Robert Ludlum?" Amy asks.

"What?" Mom looks at Amy and then at the book. "Oh, no. I'm not in to the thrillers. This is Harold's book."

Amy reaches over and checks the spine of the book. "Oh, a library book," she says. "How quaint."

"Quaint?" says my mom. "If it was a hand-copied book where the scribe had worked little animal images in to the uppercase first letter of each chapter, now *that* could be called quaint. But a paperback published in 2004, what's quaint about that?"

Amy doesn't answer her. She just gets up and puts the papers into her briefcase. "Don't bother to show me out. I know my way."

That's good because it doesn't look like anyone is planning to walk to the door with her.

"Sorry I was such a hag," Mom says as soon as the front door closes.

"Forgiven," Dad says.

"I never did like her much," I say.

"Yeah," Siobhan says to my dad. "Lucy said you probably didn't notice that Amy was acting real flirty with you."

"You noticed it too, didn't you, Mom?" I ask.

"I may have," she says. She looks at Dad. "So have I messed up a beautiful relationship for you?"

"No, I think it was the library book's fault, or maybe she was still miffed because I didn't buy in to her suggestion that the two of us should have dinner tonight to celebrate our sales deal."

"She asked you out?" I say.

"She thought I might like to take her to a five-star restaurant with a lot of ambience. I might have gone for it, but I was too embarrassed to admit I didn't have a clue which of our local eateries would qualify."

"How about Earl's?" Mom asks. By now, she's smiling a bit and looking more relaxed.

Dad just grins, shakes his head, and replies, "'fraid not."

Siobhan and I take our drinks and go back to the family room, where the dog has made herself comfortable on a chair. Mom and Dad stay at the table.

"So what are you going to buy if this sale goes through?" Mom asks.

"I was thinking about an apartment," Dad says. "How about you?"

"I might be going back to school. If I do that, I'll need to use the money from the sale to pay tuition and to live on."

"You're going to go back to school?"

"Maybe," Mom says. "Do you have a problem with that?"

"Of course not, it's your business. What are you taking?"

"That's my business too."

There's this silence that's really uncomfortable. I'm about to butt in and end the silliness, but Mom breaks down.

"Interior design. I've applied to BCIT, but I don't know if they'll accept me."

"You'd be good at that," Dad says.

"Yeah," she says. "Me and probably five hundred other applicants."

"When did you apply?"

"In February."

There's another long pause. Dad's scowling. "Why didn't you tell me? You never even told me you were thinking about it."

"Because I knew how you'd react."

"What's that supposed to mean?" Dad asks.

"I knew you'd never approve, that you'd just be so freaked out about the finances that you'd try to talk me out of it."

"So now you're a mind reader too."

"Am I wrong?"

"I don't know what I'd have done," he says. "We could never afford to have you quit your job and go to school full-time unless you agreed to sell this place, and I don't think you'd have been prepared to do that."

"What are you talking about?" she says. "I just did!"

"Because we had no choice. I know how much of yourself you put in to making this house what it is."

"You did a lot of grunt work too," Mom says.

"Yes, but it didn't matter as much to me. I'm okay with selling, but I always knew it would break your heart to lose your home."

"Who's mind reading now? We just signed the papers, and, in case you haven't noticed, my heart's still beating just fine."

She picks up her bag and grabs her keys off the table. She heads for the front door, and as she leaves she slams it a bit. Siobhan and I finally look at the TV. I turn up the volume. I have no idea what this show is about, but I suppose we have to watch it until the end so it won't be totally obvious to Dad that we've been eavesdropping.

As soon as the show is over, I tell Siobhan we need to take the dog for a walk. We're barely out the door when Siobhan says exactly what I have been thinking.

"When your mom and dad were talking about Amy, I thought they sounded really friendly."

"I'd really rather not talk about it," I say. Then I go ahead and talk about it. "It's not like I really want them fighting all the time, but, in a way, it would be easier. When they have these good moments, it gets my hopes up."

"But I don't understand what they ended up fighting about," says Siobhan.

"I don't want to talk about it," I reply. This time, that's all I say.

We walk along in silence. The dog sniffs and piddles every few feet. Walking in a new neighborhood is probably her idea of a great adventure. The street is very quiet. We don't meet a single person.

"This is a dull neighborhood, isn't it?" says Siobhan.

"Dull is good," I say. "At least I feel safe here. At my mom's place, I'm afraid to even walk the dog."

We spend most of the rest of the night talking about Brandy.

Siobhan and I sleep in on Saturday morning, probably because we stayed up way too late last night. We toast bagels for breakfast. Dad's planning to go grocery shopping this morning.

"Did Mom say when she'd be here?" I ask.

He looks confused. "She's not coming here. I'll take you home before dinner tomorrow."

"Isn't she coming to clean?"

"She doesn't have to. It looks like we have a sale on the house."

"Yeah, but how long till we move out?"

"Five weeks."

I look at the kitchen floor. I spilled a bit of the cheese topping for the popcorn last night. I noticed earlier that the microwave is dirty inside. "So what's going to happen till then?"

"Your mom wanted the place to look good so it would sell. If it's sold, I think she'll tell me what happens now is my mess and my problem."

"We should clean up," Siobhan says.

I can't believe that I go along with her plan. We spend an hour cleaning. I hope my mom appreciates our efforts. This is just *so* her job.

Dad takes us with him to the mall when he goes grocery shopping. I tell Siobhan that Dad and I don't know how to cook. We eat a lot of hot dogs, scrambled eggs, and macaroni dinners.

"Want me to show you how to make a Thai noodle salad?" she asks when we get to the store and start down the first aisle.

"Oh, Siobhan," Dad says. "I'm not in to making a fuss over cooking."

"No, really, Mr. Jensen, this recipe is dead easy."

She makes him buy bean sprouts and water chestnuts. It's almost noon when we finish. He keeps looking at his watch.

"Amy's coming by at one. I imagine we'll be out looking at apartments and houses most of the afternoon. What are you girls planning to do?"

"We could hang out at the mall," Siobhan says, "and just go window-shopping."

I have no money. How could that be fun? I go to say something, but she hits me in the ribs with her elbow.

"You sure that's okay?" Dad asks.

"Do you have enough money for lunch?" Siobhan asks me.

Dad pulls out his wallet and hands me a ten-dollar bill.

"We'll be home by four," Siobhan says.

This seems like a really stupid plan to me. But going out for lunch makes sense. We hit the McDonald's that's just a block down the street. It still leaves us a lot of time to kill. What will we do?

"Shop!" says Siobhan.

"But I have no money!"

"I don't either, but we can still shop. You just have to know how to do it."

What do I know about shopping? I come from a family where my parents don't even have a line of credit on their bank account.

We wander back to the mall. Siobhan wants to go into Mariposa.

"I guess we could look," I say as we walk into the store.

"And try things on," she adds. "That's the best part. Don't you ever imagine what it would be like to wear stuff you'd never be able to buy?"

I think of my mom's lacy push-up bra.

"Sometimes," I admit.

"So that's what we do. We each pick something we like. Then we'll go and try it on."

She's already flipping through a rack of dresses. She pulls out a polka-dotted sundress. The top part is like a skimpy halter and it ties behind the neck. The skirt starts right beneath the bra line and flares out gradually. I find the same dress in my size.

We go to the change rooms and share a stall. It's hard to believe we're trying on the same dress. Siobhan has tucked her bra straps down, and the top of the dress stretches smooth across her bust, showing off her curves. She even has cleavage. Then there's me.

"Maybe if you wore a padded bra?"

"I don't think it would fool anyone."

The dress is just hanging from the ties that are knotted behind my neck. With no boobs to fill out the top, the dress looks like a sack.

"You could try jeans under it," she says. "And a T-shirt too. Mariah has piles of these teen fashion magazines. Most of the models are thin like you, and they wear all these layers. That's the style now."

She's just trying to make me feel better, but it doesn't work.

"Mariah is lucky that Sister Alexis didn't catch her with those magazines. Can't you just imagine the lecture?"

"Oh, she didn't bring them to school," says Siobhan. "We were at her house."

I feel like someone's kicked me in the stomach. "I think I'll just go get something else," I say.

I walk out of the change room and hand the polka-dot sundress to the clerk. I go to the racks and pick up the first dress I find in my size. I don't feel like doing this anymore. I just want to go home and be by myself.

When I get back to our change room, I strip again, then pull the dress on over my head and do up the belt.

"That's better on you," Siobhan says.

"Was Janelle at Mariah's too?" I ask.

"What? Oh, you mean Wednesday when we were looking at the fashion magazines? No, it was just Mariah and me."

"I see."

Siobhan wouldn't be hanging out with Mariah if I weren't living in stupid old Langley and going to a public school named after some guy no one even remembers.

I look at Siobhan in the mirror. She's still wearing the polka-dotted sundress.

"Doesn't it make you sad to try on something that looks that good and then have to go put it back?"

"Kind of. But now let's do something different."

"What?"

She takes the dress off and puts it back on the hanger. When we've given both dresses to the clerk, we go back to the racks and Siobhan tells me the rules. We have to see who can come up with the worst outfit, or at least the outfit that looks worst on us.

That's much more fun. We're back in the change room in minutes.

Siobhan has this denim thing that's called a skirtall. The top is like the kind you see on the old farmer overalls, but the bottom's a short skirt. The material is heavy. There's a wide waistband outlined in orange thread. The skirt pockets add another horizontal line. The waistband, the pockets, and the short skirt make her hips look about ten feet wide. The bib, on the other hand, is narrow. It covers her boobs so you don't even see that they're there. The bib and the two fat straps that come up over her shoulders give her upper body a slim look, so overall she looks like a total pear. It makes me feel much better.

Then I have to try on my worst-looking outfit. I have a short plaid skirt with a wide pleated strip at the bottom. I put on a long floppy T-shirt and a sleeveless hoodie over that. You can't tell what shape I am.

We step out of our change room to see ourselves in the big mirrors.

Siobhan points to my bare legs and laughs. "You need jeans with it too. Then you'll look like the chair in my bedroom where I throw my clothes. No one will even be able to tell there's a body in there."

"Well, you should talk, you look like . . ."

We're interrupted by the sales clerk. "Is there anything I can help you with?" She's looking at me. "A smaller size in that maybe. I'll see if we have it in a size two." Then she looks at Siobhan. "That skirtall looks lovely on you, dear. It's not everyone who can wear those."

I think Siobhan's going to burst. She quickly turns her back on the clerk and says something that's probably supposed to be *thanks*, except that it comes out more like a croak.

The clerk goes out to find a smaller size for me, and Siobhan and I run back into our change room. Siobhan has her hands clamped over her mouth, trying to stifle her giggles.

I'm pulling off all the clothes I have on. She starts to unhook the big metal hooks on the straps of her skirtall.

"You're not planning to put that back, are you, dear?" I say. "It looks so lovely on you."

Then we both are laughing so hard we have to hang on to each other or we'll fall over.

The clerk comes back with a smaller T-shirt for me. She doesn't seem so friendly anymore.

"I think we maybe need to get out of here," Siobhan says.

I think she's right.

fifteen

I make dinner. No one who knows me would ever believe it. Siobhan just sits on the stool by the island and tells me what to do. She writes down the recipe so I can do it myself some other time too. I boil ramen noodles for three minutes and then drain them and let them cool. All I have to do is add veggies and slivered almonds and it's a Thai noodle salad. For the dressing, I mix the flavor package from the noodles with some oil and vinegar. It's very easy, but it tastes fancy. Dad's impressed.

I ask him if he saw any interesting places when he was out with Amy this afternoon.

He just shrugs. "Nothing to get excited about."

Siobhan has called her mom and she's allowed to come to mass with us tonight. I've told her about the choir. When Father Tony gets that youth group going in September, he says it will probably meet after the

Saturday night mass, so Siobhan says she wants to scope out Father Tony, the choir, and any kids our age who might be there.

We get there early, which is maybe not such a great idea. Catholics don't talk in church. We're supposed to be praying, or at least being quiet so other people can pray. The trouble with being quiet is that it gives me time to think about all the things I've managed to forget while Siobhan and I have been together today. Things like Brandy. Things like my mom going out with Jake. Things like never being able to go back to Holy Name because my mom is probably going to need all her money for her own school fees. The longer I kneel there, the worse I feel. What have I done to deserve this? I'm not that bad a person.

I glance back over my shoulder. The light is on outside the confession room; the door is open. Maybe Father Tony has some ideas about what I can do about Brandy.

I lean over to Siobhan and whisper, "I'm going to go to confession."

"Why? Do you think trying on clothes when we weren't going to buy anything . . . do you think that's a sin?"

I hadn't even thought about that. I shake my head. "No, it's more that I need some spiritual direction."

Almost all the saints had spiritual directors, someone you can tell all your troubles to, and then they're supposed to give you guidance. I could really use some guidance, especially about Brandy.

I walk to the confession room. When I go in, I can't see Father Tony because he's sitting behind a screen. That's how it's supposed to be. There's a kneeler on my side of the screen, so if I didn't want the priest to see me, I could just kneel there and then sneak out when I was finished and he'd never know it was me. At least that's the theory. Grandma always goes behind the screen, even though she's almost best friends with Father Mac. He must know her voice by now.

Most younger people don't bother with the screen and instead talk face-to-face. I walk past the screen and sit in the chair that's opposite Father Tony.

He makes the sign of the cross over me.

"Bless me, Father, for I have sinned. It's been . . ." I'm supposed to tell him how long it's been since my last confession. Did I go during Lent? I must have. "About three months, I think . . ."

He doesn't say anything. Usually the priest waits until the end.

"I accuse myself of the following sins." I should have thought about this more. I haven't done a proper examination of my conscience. I was mostly thinking of all my problems. "I do not love this girl Brandy as much as a Christian should. Actually, I don't love her at all. I don't even like her." I pause.

Father Tony is looking down at his hands, which are folded in his lap. He's still listening.

"I was very rude to my mom's friend Gina, and to Mom too. I never understand that commandment. I know

I'm supposed to honor my mother, but what if she's planning to do something really bad?"

Maybe because I make it a question, this time he says something.

"Saint Augustine tells us we're to hate the sin but love the sinner. I think it's like that when we're talking about respecting our parents. You honor your mother because she gave you life. That doesn't mean you have to approve of everything she does."

"Well, I certainly don't approve of her going out with Jake next weekend. She's a married woman. That's a mortal sin. I do love her, you know. I don't want her to go straight to hell."

"I wouldn't worry about that, Lucy. It isn't a sin for her to go out with a friend, even if it's a male friend."

"Could I go to hell because I hate Brandy?"

"God isn't quick to throw people into hell. Where do you get these ideas from anyway?"

"Grandma has a lot of old books. Have you read about the visions those kids saw in Fatima? All those flames and people screaming?"

"Yes, I've read it. But they were visions, you know, not the real thing. Let's forget about hell for a bit and talk about Brandy."

That's about the same thing if you ask me. "What about her?" I ask.

"Well," he says, "what is she like?"

"She's much bigger than me, and she has black hair with blue streaks in it."

"But what kind of a person is she?"

"Mean! She's always pushing me around and calling me names. If she ever catches me alone, she'll probably beat me up."

"Has she said anything that might give a clue as to why she's picking on you?"

"First time she laid eyes on me, she said I should go to the elementary school."

He nods.

"Then I asked the teacher about something in class, and after that, it got really bad. She thought I was sucking up to the teacher."

"What sort of a student is Brandy?"

"A bad one. She doesn't do her work half the time."

"Do you think she might be jealous because you're a good student?"

I don't believe it for a minute, but I don't want to sound rude. "I guess it's possible," I say.

"Maybe you could help her."

I think there's something to be said for the idea of letting priests get married. Maybe they should also have regular jobs, like some protestant ministers do. It would help them get a grip on reality. The problem with priests spending all their time praying and saying masses is that they haven't a clue about what life is really about. I can't believe this man is suggesting that I help Brandy with her homework.

"It's not that I wouldn't be willing, but there's no

way that's going to happen." What part of "she'll probably beat me up" doesn't he get?

"Is there anything more you have to confess, Lucy?"

"I can't think of anything."

"For your penance, say a prayer for Brandy each
morning and night this coming week, and I want you to
watch her closely. See if there's any way you could show
love toward her, even if you don't feel it."

Father Mac always gives me Hail Marys or Our Fathers
to pray. What kind of a penance is this? "Yes, Father."

"And now I absolve you of all your sins, in the name
of the Father, and of the Son, and of the Holy Spirit.
Go in the peace of Christ."

When I get back to the pew, I kneel down to do the
first part of my penance. I try to think of something to
pray about for Brandy. My mind is blank at first. I wonder
why God makes people mean like that. That is the clue,
I think. God did make her, and He can't want her to be
the kind of person she is.

I bow my head and pray, "Our Father in heaven,
look down with favor on your child Brandy. You've got
to be able to do something with her."

The choir is starting up for the opening hymn. I
make the sign of the cross and stand up to sing with
Siobhan and Dad.

When Dad takes me home Sunday afternoon, Gina's
car is parked in front of our trailer. No wonder Ian

doesn't marry her. She never stays home. I lift the dog out of the van and carry her into the trailer. I put her down just inside the door, and go to my room to take off my backpack. By the time I get back to the kitchen, Gina has picked the dog up and has her on her lap. I pretend I don't notice.

"Have a good weekend?" I ask Mom.

"Quiet."

I look in the fridge to see if there's something to drink. I find a little can of juice.

"Gina and Ian have found a town house," Mom says.

My heart stops. I make myself take a breath. I don't faint or anything, so I guess my heart must have started up again.

"Three bedrooms," says Gina. "And Ian won't have an excuse for not helping me cook or do dishes anymore. The kitchen is big enough for two people."

And I suppose they allow dogs.

"So, when are you moving?" I ask.

"The end of May."

I just nod. The dog is still on her lap. "I've got homework I should do." I start toward my bedroom. There is a small thud and the scratching of little dog nails on the kitchen linoleum. The dog's jumped off Gina's knee; she follows me into my room.

I close the door behind us, but not before I hear Gina say, "So much for dogs being loyal. I think my Lucy's getting so she likes your Lucy better than she likes me."

And so she should. I wouldn't just dump her with

someone else so I could go live with a boyfriend. Gina expects us to treat the dog like a lamp or a coffee table that we've been storing for her. As soon as she moves to her new town house, she'll want her "property" back.

I'm depressed all evening. At bedtime, I'm so busy praying for the dog that I almost forget I'm supposed to pray for Brandy. When I remember, I just ask God to make her a nicer person.

sixteen

God must have his own ideas about how to fix things. I don't know if Brandy is any nicer on Monday, but she isn't at school, and that makes it way nicer for me. What I'd really like to pray for is that she'd disappear completely, but I don't think that's what Father Tony had in mind when he gave me this penance. Still, it's such a relief not having her around. I get to walk home from school without going blocks out of the way.

I'm in a good mood when I get home from school. I even make dinner. My mom is really surprised when she comes home and I have a Thai noodle salad all ready to dish up. She's especially surprised because we didn't have any bean sprouts or water chestnuts in the house.

"I planned it all yesterday," I say. "I borrowed the stuff I needed from Dad's place."

"Does he know?"

"I'm not sure."

"Well, it's very good," she says. "And it's such a luxury to come home and find dinner is all ready."

After we clean up, Mom is sitting at the table, going over her bills again. She has this pad of yellow lined paper and she's written numbers and lists on its pages.

"Those people accepted our counteroffer today."

"So that means the house is sold?"

She nods. We both look sad.

"When do we have to move out?"

"June 15."

She goes back to her figures. I'm thinking about what Amy said, about how the house prices are going up so fast that if Mom doesn't buy another house right away, she won't ever be able to afford one. What if we have to live here forever and I never get away from Brandy?

"Dad was looking at places again Saturday," I say.

"Did he see anything he liked?"

"Have you heard about those zero lot line houses? There's a bunch of them off Eightieth Avenue. They're two storeys but kind of narrow. The lots are only thirty-three feet wide."

"I thought he said he was going to get an apartment."

"He might, but now he's saying maybe he'll buy a house and rent it out, and then just rent an apartment for himself."

She's looking at her budget pages and twirling her hair around her pencil. "I'm going to use up all of my money from the house just on living expenses. Gas prices are nuts. It costs me fifty dollars to fill my tank now. And look at this hydro bill. It costs as much for this little place as it did for our house, and our trailer is, what? Three or four times smaller?"

"That makes no sense."

"I know it doesn't. The weather's been mild; we don't have the heat on that much."

"Have you thought it might be something that Randy has in the shed?" I ask.

"Oh, Lucy, will you quit going on about the shed. He's not heating that space."

"But maybe he has some really strong lights in there."

"I know what you're thinking," she says, "but you can forget it. If he were growing marijuana, we'd smell it. That stuff stinks to high heaven."

And since when was she an expert on drugs? Later I take the dog out for her bedtime pee. When I come back, I walk around to the back of the shed. I press my ear to the door. I can hear a humming noise. I move around to the side that faces Mrs. Warren's trailer. The humming is louder.

"What are you doing?" a voice asks.

Mrs. Warren has opened the small window over her kitchen sink.

"Something's humming in there."

"You don't know what it is?"

"No. Randy, our landlord, he keeps stuff in there."

"What kind of stuff?"

"That's what I'd like to know."

"I'd tell your mother to check that out, if I were you." She closes the window with a bit of a slam.

I don't tell Mom. What's the point? She'd just ignore me or tell me to mind my own business.

That night, I have to pray for Brandy again. Whoever heard of a penance that takes all week to do? By the time I finish the penance, I'll probably have committed a bunch more sins. Anyway, this time I try something a little different. I ask God to help Brandy with whatever the problem is that is making her so crabby and mean.

She's not at school the next day, or the day after that.

Harbie and Kuldeep and I talk about it at lunch on Wednesday.

"Maybe she's moved," I say.

"Or she might be sick."

"More likely skipping out," says Kuldeep. "I have math with her, and she didn't have her homework done last class."

"Well, that's not such a big deal," I say.

"For Brandy it is," says Kuldeep. "She's on probation."

I almost choke on my chocolate milk. "What did she do?"

I can just guess. Probably a really serious assault on whoever it was she hated most before she met me.

"Not like probation with the police," says Kuldeep. "She was suspended for skipping and not doing any homework. I hear they let her come back to school but only on sort of a trial basis. If she starts goofing off again, she'll be expelled."

That doesn't help me. Even if she gets kicked out of school, I'll still always have to worry about meeting up with her around the trailer park. I'm just hoping she's moved, maybe to Toronto or Halifax.

But she hasn't. She's back at school Thursday, making rude comments to me in English class and bumping in to me "by accident" in the halls. I take the long route home after school and make it there without seeing her, but I have to take the dog out for at least a bit of a walk. I try to stay as close to our place as I can, so I just walk down the road, past a couple of trailers, and turn around to come back. Suddenly Brandy's right there. She's come out of nowhere. I almost bump into her.

She looks as surprised as I feel, but it only takes her a minute to regain her composure.

"What are *you* doing here, bitch?"

"I live here."

She looks around like she's never seen the place before. "In this dump? I picked you for one of those snobby Greenwood Glade or Paradise Ridge types."

I wonder how she guessed that that's where we used to live. I don't ask her. I just keep my mouth shut. She's between me and our trailer.

Then she looks down at the dog.

"What the hell's that supposed to be? I hate those little kick dogs. Good for nothing. If I got a dog, it would be a real one."

She takes a couple of steps toward us, so I bend over and pick the dog up in a hurry. The dog's not stupid.

She knows a mean person when she sees one. She starts to bark.

Brandy just laughs. She takes another step toward me; her hands are still at her sides, but they're clenched into fists. I take a step back.

"Oh, that's sure a scary dog," she says in this sarcastic voice.

The dog is going crazy. I'm struggling to keep hold of her.

"I could punch you out and leave you bleeding and unconscious if I weren't so afraid of your big, fierce guard dog."

"Enough!" someone yells in a scratchy old-lady voice.

Mrs. Warren is standing on her porch with her phone in her hand.

"If I hit one more number, the cops will be on their way. You get home."

Brandy gives her the finger, but she turns and heads back the way she must have come. I'm just sweating like crazy.

"Thanks," I say.

"How long has this been going on?" Mrs. Warren asks.

"Since the very first day I started school here. I don't know why she hates me."

"You better come in and stay with me till your mom comes home. I don't like the idea of you staying alone."

I don't like the idea much myself.

"But what about the dog?"

"It can wait here too. I like animals."

I should have guessed that, what with all the pig knickknacks she has around the place. The inside of her trailer is even more cluttered with them than the outside. They are on her dish towels and pot holders. She has a wallpaper border of cheerful-looking pink pigs all around the kitchen and living room area. She's putting tea bags into a teapot shaped like a pig that's sitting up like a dog might. She has a whole shelf unit filled with nothing but piggy banks.

"Wow! What a collection."

"Yeah, I've got eight hundred and seventy-three pigs if you count pictures like the ones embroidered on the cushions and the dish towels."

"How long have you been collecting them?"

"I started when Herb passed on."

"Was Herb your husband?"

"Yes, he passed away in 2001."

The kettle is boiling. She pours the water into the teapot.

"Do you mind if I use your phone?" I ask. "I always call my grandma when I get home from school. I don't want her worrying about me."

"You go ahead and call her then."

I key in Grandma's number, but no one answers. I wonder where she's off to this time. Bridge again? But then where's Granddad?

Mrs. Warren and I are watching *Charlotte's Web* on video when my mom pulls in. I go outside to tell her that Mrs. Warren and I are watching a movie. She says

I can stay until it's finished.

Dinner's almost ready when I get home.

"So, since when were you and Mrs. Warren friends?" Mom asks.

I tell her what happened with Brandy while we're eating.

"This is getting really serious. I wish Mrs. Warren had called the police. Maybe they'd have been able to do something about her."

"Father Tony says I should pray for her."

"Well, that's fine, but it's not keeping you safe right now."

That's something I never understand about God. You're supposed to have faith and all that, but He is *so* slow.

"I wish we had a cell phone," Mom says. "We could program it to call 911. I wonder what they cost."

"Forget it. It would be a waste of money. Brandy would probably send it flying with her first punch. I'd never get it to my ear."

Mom starts clearing away our dishes. "I wish I didn't have to go out tomorrow night. You'll just have to promise me you'll stay inside and keep the door locked."

She's at the sink, and it's like she's purposely keeping busy so she doesn't have to look at me.

"I'll walk the dog before I leave," she says.

"Where are you going? I can't stay here alone. Why can't I come with you?"

"I've got to go out for my big date with Jake." She makes quotation marks in the air with her fingers when she says the word *date*. "I've already made a complete fool of myself by nodding my head at the wrong time, it seems. If I show up for our date with you in tow, that would be just way too embarrassing."

"Don't go out with him at all. Just tell him you didn't hear him properly, and, if you had, the answer would have been no. What's so hard about that?"

"I don't want to hurt his feelings. I mean, he's been quite nice. He helped us move and everything. It's not his fault that I'm deaf."

"But you shouldn't be going out on dates."

"I'll just go out for dinner with him, and, while we're eating, I can explain my mistake in a funny way. Then I'll pay my part of the bill and come home. I won't be late at all."

"But I'm scared to stay here alone. Why can't I go to Dad's a day early, like I did last week?"

"So what do I tell him? 'Can Lucy stay with you, I have a date'?"

"Well, that's the truth."

"I'd really rather he didn't know."

"Then I'll call Grandma," I say.

"She and Granddad have gone to the Skagit Valley Casino. They won't be back till Sunday."

I am totally shocked. "I didn't know she was going away. She's never gone away without me before."

"She could hardly be expected to take you to a casino."

"But she didn't even tell me she was going."

"It was kind of a last-minute plan. You talk to her every single day. I find it hard to believe she wouldn't have mentioned it."

"I don't talk to her every single day. She's out half the time, and I do have a life of my own, you know. Have you forgotten I was busy making dinner Tuesday night? I can't always be on the phone."

"I suppose you could invite Siobhan over. Would that help?" Mom asks.

I'd really rather go to Siobhan's so I'm as far away as possible from Brandy. "That would be better than being alone," I say.

I call Siobhan and ask her if she wants to get together tomorrow night. I'm hoping she'll invite me to her place, but right away she says she'll ask her mom if she can come over. The trouble is, Siobhan thinks it's a big treat any time she can get away from all those little kids.

She's back on the line in half a minute. "Mom says I can come for the evening, but I can't stay over. She needs me to babysit first thing Saturday morning."

"That should be okay," I say. "My mom says she'll be home really early anyway."

Mom raises her eyebrows at me.

"If Siobhan's dad drops her off tomorrow, can you take her home after?" I ask Mom.

"Sure. Like you say, I'll be home *really* early."

seventeen

om drives me to school on Friday, and at lunchtime, I get called to the office because there's a message for me to phone her at work. When I get through, she tells me that she has made arrangements to work through her lunch hour so she can get off an hour early. She won't make it to the school until almost four, but she says I can wait in the library. That's not a place where Brandy is likely to be hanging out, so I give a big sigh of relief.

When we get home, Mom makes homemade pizza so that all Siobhan and I will have to do is pop it in the oven. After Siobhan arrives, Mom walks the dog and then goes over to see Mrs. Warren. When she comes back, she says Mrs. Warren will watch out for me, and if I have any problems, I can call her.

About six-thirty, Jake shows up. He looks like he's just had a shower. He's dressed nicely. I hate him. See, that's another sin, and I'm not even going to finish my penance from last week until bedtime tonight.

"He is so hot," Siobhan says as soon as they leave. She can't take her eyes off him. I'm surprised she doesn't press her nose right up against the window and stare like a kid looking into a candy store.

"Get a grip," I say.

I check the clock. It's 6:35. Mom says she'll be home by nine. She better be.

It's a good thing Siobhan's over. It's hard to keep worrying when she's around. She is a very distracting person, in a good sort of way. She says she has plans for us, a surprise. She won't tell me until we finish eating and cleaning up. Then she goes into her backpack and pulls out a white plastic bag.

"Look what I bought."

She opens the bag and a box of Born to be Blonde hair dye and two packages of strawberry-flavored Kool-Aid fall out onto the table.

"We're going to do makeovers." Siobhan's got long, wavy hair. It used to be really blonde, but it's getting darker. "You can put in highlights for me."

I read the instructions. It doesn't sound hard. There are plastic gloves in the box. I get out the bleaching gel and the bottle of toner. There's a plastic cap and something that looks like a crochet hook. I look at the instructions again.

"Should I wash my hair first?" Siobhan asks.

"No, just sit down. We have to get this cap on your head."

It takes me quite awhile to pull little strands of Siobhan's hair through the holes in the plastic cap. I try to be gentle, but with long hair, it snarls sometimes, so I have to tug a bit. Siobhan is gritting her teeth. Her eyes are red and watery.

Once we think we have enough hair pulled through the cap, I paint the strands with the gel and set the timer on the stove. When it goes off, we rinse out the gel and put the toner on. Getting the cap off is another major production. When we're finished, Siobhan washes her hair and uses the blow-dryer. It looks so cool. It's a really professional-looking job, if I do say so myself. Siobhan loves it.

"Now it's your turn," she says. "Look, I bought Kool-Aid. We can give you pink streaks. It will make your hair way more interesting."

"I wouldn't mind being blonde too," I say.

"Well, I couldn't afford two packages of the real hair color. This is the best I could do. Are you going to try it or not?"

"I'll try it."

"We need hair conditioner."

I go to the bathroom and come back with the bottle. Siobhan pours a little bit into a saucer and mixes in the packages of Kool-Aid.

We don't use the cap or the crochet hook for me. Siobhan just brushes the colored paste she's made through a strand here and a strand there. When she's finished, I check it out in the mirror. I don't like it as much as Siobhan's. Hers looks natural. Mine looks kind of fun, though, and it will wash out after awhile.

There's some of the Kool-Aid mix left over.

"We should give the dog some streaks too," Siobhan says. "She's feeling left out."

Anytime anyone says *dog*, the dog gets all excited, so now she is bouncing around my legs. I pick her up and hold her while Siobhan puts pink streaks in her fur. The dog panics when I try to use the blow-dryer on her, so we just leave her to dry on her own.

Mom comes in at 8:45. We've cleaned everything up and we're just watching TV.

"How did it go?" I ask.

"It was okay. He was a good sport about it. He said he was just disappointed he'd changed his sheets for nothing. Can you believe that?"

"Mom!" I'm totally shocked.

How can she say something like that to me, especially in front of Siobhan? I turn to glare at her, but she's staring hard at me. The room is pretty dim. We only have one lamp and the TV on. She switches on the overhead light in the kitchen.

"Oh my God!"

"Mom, you shouldn't say *God* like that."

She looks at Siobhan. "Your mother's going to kill me."

Still, Mom doesn't look that worried about it. Actually, she looks like she wants to laugh.

Then she notices the dog. "Not you too!" And then she really does laugh.

Siobhan's mother, whose name is Colleen, does not kill my mom. What she says, though, is that Siobhan can't come over anymore because my mom is single and dating and she isn't able to properly supervise us.

Siobhan tells me the news when she calls me early the next morning.

My mom gets pretty annoyed when I tell her.

"What a hypocrite," she says. "They leave Siobhan there on her own with those kids all the time. You've been over at Siobhan's when her parents have gone out."

eighteen

The next day, Dad takes me to see the zero lot line house he told me about last weekend. It's a really run-down dump of a place near the end of a cul-de-sac. The only nice thing about the place is the street it's on. There's a grassy island in the middle of the loop where the cars have to go round the circle and turn back. It's almost like a very little park because they've planted three ornamental cherry trees in there. It would be a good place to walk a dog. All the houses on the street are about the same size and are on small lots, but they're fixed up and look kind of cute. Dad says the house we're checking out is about the cheapest one in all of Surrey. I'm not surprised.

It looks so sad and abandoned. No one's living in it. The yard is a jungle. There's a strip of cracked pavement with weeds growing through it that leads right up to the base of the house. You can tell this is where the garage used to be, but now it's closed in and there's a boarded up window. Dad tells me this is the family room. There are shards of broken glass on the ground.

Amy's late. She's supposed to meet us here. Dad has been through the house once but wants to have a second look. I can't believe he's seriously considering this place. We're standing by the curb, waiting, when one of the neighbors comes over.

"Hi there," he says. "Roy's the name."

Dad introduces himself and me.

"Are you planning to buy? I sure hope so. It would be such a relief to have someone normal in here."

"We're still just checking things out," Dad says.

I like the way he says *we*, like I'll have some say in the decision. I wish. This place is a dump, but it's not that far from Siobhan's, and if I lived here, Grandma could drive me to Holy Name. If Dad wanted me to make a decision, what would I say?

"Sure would be great if we could get a nice family in here," Roy says. "This is a real family neighborhood." He sort of waves his arm in an arc to indicate all the houses where there are bikes and toys in the driveways.

"That's kind of what appeals to us," says Dad. "But there's a lot of work to do here. The place is in rough shape."

"Yeah, I know. Guy who owns it lives in Hong Kong. Tried renting it out. It was a really ugly scene. One group of young guys after another. Police were always here. Nice to have a crack house in the neighborhood, eh? The rest of us got together and pretty well drove them out."

Dad looks alarmed. "Is the person who buys it going to have members of the old crowd turning up on their doorstep?"

"Nah. Cops busted it months ago, and the owner's just left it empty. He's trying to sell it, but look at the shape it's in. It's a fixer-upper special now. He's dropped his price a couple of times."

Amy pulls up and parks out on the street. She's going to show us through the house.

"Well, I'll leave you to look it over then," Roy says, and he wanders back across the road to his own house.

Amy's starting her sales spiel. "Of course, this place needs a little TLC, but you can see that it has great potential."

About as much potential as a chicken coop. I don't see any at all. It's a dive, plain and simple.

The living room and the dining room have hardwood floors, but they're all stained and scratched. There's a hole in the drywall in the kitchen, like someone's punched the wall or thrown something at it. The kitchen cabinets are all scuffed up, and some of the doors don't hang straight. There are burn holes in the countertop. The stove is crusted with food. I don't know how they can expect to sell a house in this condition. Who'd buy it?

Apparently my dad might. This is his second time looking it over, and it's not like he's having Amy show him any other places today. He actually seems to be interested in this one.

I can't wait to tell Siobhan, so as soon as we get home, I call her. She isn't in. Her mom says she's at Megan's. Who's Megan?

Siobhan finally calls me back.

"Your mom says you were at Megan's place," I say. "Who's Megan?"

"She just moved in down at the Carlsons' place."

"Which place is the Carlsons'?"

"The one two doors down from us, toward the park. She's a foster kid. The Carlsons just got approved to run some sort of a group home. They're only taking teenage girls. They can have up to three, but right now, there's just Megan."

"So why's she in a foster home?"

"Her mother's in rehab."

"What's she like? Megan, I mean, not her mother."

"Funny! She's got a wicked sense of humor. I haven't laughed so hard in my life. And it's so nice that she lives right on my own street. It's always such a major production when you and I want to get together."

"Well, I wouldn't call it a major production. Dad says he'll come and pick you up, if you want to come over."

"That would be cool. I'll ask my mom."

She does come over, and she even stays the night, but it still bothers me that all week I'm going to be out in Langley and Megan is only going to be two houses away. It's pretty obvious who Siobhan is going to be spending more time with. There's no justice. Why is it that when Siobhan meets a girl her age that lives close to her, it's someone who is a lot of fun. When I meet a girl my age that lives close to me, she's a weirdo who wants to beat me to a pulp.

With Mom driving me to and from school, and me making sure I'm never out alone, Brandy doesn't have much of a chance to actually kill me. She can still bug me at school, though. I hate it that she sits right behind me in English class. I keep expecting to get a knife shoved between my shoulder blades. What happens Monday isn't quite that bad, but it's close enough to almost give me a heart attack.

"All right, now last class we were talking about similes and metaphors. I asked each of you to pick a poem you liked and to look for the imagery the poet used." Ms. Phillips looks around the class. No one has put up their hand. "No volunteers?" She looks straight at me; no, she's looking over me.

Suddenly I get this really hard poke in the middle of my back.

"Put your hand up!" Brandy hisses.

I don't even think. Up my hand goes like Brandy's put a gun in my back. I'm surprised I don't throw both arms up into the air.

"Yes, Lucy," Ms. Phillips says.

"I picked 'Fog,'" I say. "By Carl Sandburg." It takes me a minute to collect my thoughts. "He compared fog to a cat. It's not a simile, I don't think, because there's no *like* or *as* in it."

I try to explain. Ms. Phillips asks me to read it aloud. Then she asks questions. Anyone can answer, but it's mostly me who does the talking. We're still discussing it when the bell rings.

I'm gathering up my things, but Brandy's faster than me. As she walks by my desk, she looks down and says, "I knew you had to be good for something." Then she just walks out of the room.

If it wasn't for the way she usually treats me, I'd almost think she gave a bit of a smile when she said that. Maybe it was just a grimace.

I'm about to describe what happened with Brandy in class to Harbie and Kuldeep, who are sitting in the cafeteria, but I don't get a chance.

"Your hair," says Harbie as I approach their table. "I still can't believe what you did to your hair."

"My parents would kill me if I did that," says Kuldeep.

Kuldeep and Harbie have been going on like this about my hair for a week now. You'd think I'd shaved my head bald or something. I wish they'd just get over it.

It turns out, though, that they aren't the only ones who get totally bent out of shape over a little change in hair color. Tuesday night, Ian has a meeting and so Gina comes over to visit Mom. I know she's coming because probably for the first time in her life she calls first. As soon as her car pulls in to the driveway, the dog starts barking. The dog's still at it when Gina walks in the door, so it's not like Gina isn't going to notice her right away. And she does. She stops right inside the door and stares.

"What have you done to my dog?" she shrieks.

Gina's just standing there like she's paralyzed. Her hands have flown to her cheeks. She's looking at the dog as if this is the worst thing she's ever seen. The dog is probably stunned by the response. She quits barking.

"She looks ridiculous."

"It's just Kool-Aid," I say. "It will wash out in a bit."

"I'm not going to be seen walking down the street with a striped dog."

And when was the last time you walked this poor dog anywhere, I want to ask.

"I just won't put myself through that humiliation," she says. "I'm sorry, Lucy, but you and your mom will just have to keep her."

She's looking at my mom. Mom's smiling. I look back at Gina. She is too. I look at the dog.

"We can keep her?" I can't believe my ears.

"Well, if you want her," Gina says. "Not everyone would want a silly little dog with pink-striped fur."

I pick up the dog and bury my face in her neck. "I would."

It feels like a big weight has lifted off my shoulders. I don't know what to say. I've been so awful to Gina. The dog is wriggling. I set her down.

"Thank you," I say. I'm smiling now too, but it's a wobbly sort of smile. Then, like an idiot, I throw my arms around Gina's neck and start to bawl. "Thank you, thank you, thank you. I'll take real good care of her."

"I know that," says Gina.

When I calm myself down enough to notice, I see that Gina and Mom are looking a little teary eyed too. We exchange looks, and then we all start to laugh. The dog just stands there watching us and wagging her tail.

nineteen

When we get home on Thursday afternoon, there is a letter from BCIT in our mailbox. Mom doesn't open it right away. It sits there on the kitchen table while she makes dinner. It sits there on the kitchen table while we eat dinner. It sits there on the kitchen table while we do dishes. The suspense is driving me crazy.

"Why don't you open it?" I ask for the third time.

"I'm afraid to," Mom says.

"I'll open it for you."

"No, leave it alone. I'll open it in a minute."

After we finish at the sink, she goes and sits at the table and stares at the envelope like she thinks maybe it contains anthrax or something like that.

"As long as I hadn't heard from them, at least I could hope," she says. But while she's saying that, she's finally started to work her thumb under the edge of the flap on the envelope. She goes through the process of opening the envelope, unfolding the single sheet of paper, and smoothing the letter out on the table – all in slow motion. Finally, she starts reading it.

I sit down across from her holding my breath the whole time. She's so slow, it's a wonder I don't collapse. The thing is, I don't even know what I hope the letter says. I know she really wants to take this interior design course, and so I sort of hope she gets in. But on the other hand, I really want to move, and there's a better chance of that happening if she doesn't get in.

She's finished reading. She just sits there, staring at me. Then suddenly she shrieks! It startles me so much I just about hit the roof. She grabs my hands and pulls me up.

"I got in! I got in!" She's dancing us both in circles around our little kitchen, screaming like a mad woman.

I can't help laughing. "Mom! You keep this yelling up and Mrs. Warren will call the police."

Mom is laughing and crying at the same time. "I don't care. Nothing would bother me tonight."

Mom drives me over to Dad's after school on Friday. She and Dad have things they have to discuss.

Dad's made tea and he's bought some Nanaimo bars. I help myself. He pours tea in Mom's cup and then his own.

"You don't realize how much stuff you've

accumulated till you're faced with the job of having to move it all," he says. "We need to come up with a plan so we know who's taking what."

"Lucy tells me at least you are going to have a house to move into," Mom says.

"I'm not moving to the house; I've rented an apartment in Burnaby."

Mom turns to me. "I thought you said Dad was buying a house off Eightieth Avenue."

"I am," he says. "But I won't be living there. I'll be renting it out."

"And then you're renting an apartment?" Mom looks puzzled.

"Well, I thought it would make sense to move closer to my job, but I sure couldn't afford to buy anything in Vancouver or Burnaby."

"So this house you're buying is just sort of an investment?"

Dad nods.

"I got in to that course I was telling you about," Mom says. She doesn't sound excited about it at all tonight. Mostly she just looks worried.

"Well, good for you," Dad says. "So will you be staying where you are or moving closer in?"

"I don't know what I'm doing," she says.

She can say that again. I've asked her about a million times and she won't even discuss it with me. My whole life is in limbo.

"The thing is, the rent's so cheap there and it's close

to the freeway, so the commute to BCIT wouldn't take that much longer than if we lived here."

"So it would make sense for you to stay where you are then."

"In some ways, but has Lucy told you about Brandy?" Mom asks.

I haven't, so she does. Dad's scowling while she talks; it gets worse when Mom tells the part about Mrs. Warren having to rescue me.

"I've been driving her to school, and since this happened, I've arranged to work through my lunch hour so I can come home early and pick her up from school."

"But it's not safe for her to go out of the house, even to walk the dog," Dad says.

It's not a question.

Dad stares into his tea for a second or two. Then he says, "Do you mind telling me how much you're paying for rent where you are?"

"I can't really see that that is any of your business," Mom says.

"Five hundred dollars a month," I say.

"How much did Lucy tell you about the place I'm buying?" he asks.

"Everything," I say. "I told her it was an abandoned crack house on a nice street. That Roy's not going to be very happy when he finds out you're going to be renting it out again."

"It looks rough, but I'm taking two weeks' holiday as soon as I take possession, and I think I can get it fixed up in that amount of time. Lucy's right, though, Roy and the other neighbors will be very upset if I don't choose really responsible renters."

"Look," says Mom. "Shouldn't we get down to discussing what we're going to do with all our furniture? We do have to be out of this house in just over two weeks. And that's why I came over."

"How do you know what furniture you want to take when you don't know where you're going to be living?" I ask.

"Well, that's the point I was trying to get to," says Dad. "Kate, why don't you rent this house I'm buying? I'll let you have it for five hundred dollars a month."

This is an excellent idea.

"No," she says.

"But Mom! It would be perfect. It's quite close to Siobhan's, and it's not so far from Grandma and Granddad's, so Grandma could drive me to Holy Name like before."

"No," she says again. "Thanks for the offer, Harold, but I'm not comfortable accepting favors like that."

"You never think of anyone but yourself!" I yell.

She doesn't even bother to yell back. She just picks up her jacket and walks out. I feel like kicking holes in our walls. Instead, I run up to my room and pound cushions and scream as loudly as I can into my pillows.

When I calm down, I try to call Siobhan.

Her mom says that Siobhan has gone to a movie with Megan.

I throw myself down on the bed again and scream into my pillows until I'm hoarse.

It's almost bedtime before I go back downstairs. Dad is sitting at the computer playing FreeCell.

"You never did decide how to split up the furniture," I say.

"Maybe we'll just have to see if we can get one of those auction houses to sell it," he replies. "If you're going to stay in the trailer and I'm in a one-bedroom apartment, neither of us will have room for much of it."

I'm so mad at my mom that I don't even want to go back to her place on Sunday night, but what choice do I have? None, just like always. I'm so depressed that if I weren't Catholic, I would seriously be considering suicide. I spend the whole week trying to think of a way out of this horrible trailer.

It's Thursday night and I'm taking the dog for the world's shortest walk. I have to stay within sight of our trailer so Mom can come rescue me if Brandy sees me. Mrs. Warren calls me over. She asks if I told my mom about the humming noise coming from our shed.

I confess that I haven't. "I don't think she'd listen to me. I mean, she was complaining about how high the hydro bill was, and I said it might be because Randy had something in that shed that was using a lot of electricity."

"What did she say about that?"

"She just says it's none of our business what he stores in his shed."

"Humph," she says, and she walks back into her trailer.

It's hard to tell sometimes whether an idea comes from God or from the devil. That's how I feel when we walk into English class one day and I hear Brandy talking to her friends. She's in a total panic. She's supposed to be doing a book report – out loud, in front of the whole class. She's only read the first thirty pages of the book.

"Crap," she says. "I might as well not even sit down. I might as well just go to the principal's office right now so he can call my mom and tell her I'm kicked out again. Watch me, I'll be grounded all friggin' summer."

She crashes her books down on the desk behind me. I sneak a peek. She's sitting with her head resting on top of them.

Ms. Phillips comes in. I don't think I'm really the teacher's pet like Brandy's always saying, but Ms. Phillips does like me. Mostly I think she gets bored teaching kids who aren't interested in English. She always gets quite excited if I ask questions and we get to talking about some poem or story in more detail. A couple of times, I've distracted her so badly that she and I have spent the whole period talking while everyone else sat around looking bored. Usually when I realize what I've done, I feel guilty. I thinks she feels guilty too, for ignoring all her other students.

"Today," she says, "we're going to wrap up our poetry unit and then Brandy and Greg are going to do their book reports for us."

She gives us some notes about the last three poems in the unit. There aren't that many, so we copy them from the overhead. When most of us have put down our pens, she looks around the classroom.

"Is everyone finished?" she asks.

I stick my hand up.

"Yes, Lucy."

"This is going to sound like a really stupid question," I say.

She nods. Some of the other kids sigh and roll their eyes.

"How can you tell if a piece is even a poem?"

"What do you mean?"

"Well, the old poems all rhyme and have sort of a beat. Nowadays, poems aren't like that. Like that one you read us about the plums."

"You mean, 'This Is Just to Say'?"

"Whatever. He just says he ate the plums she was wanting for breakfast and that they were delicious. There's no rhyme, there's no rhythm; there are no similes or metaphors. There are just short lines."

She nods. People around me yawn.

"So what about if I leave my mom a note that says 'Gone to the mall, Shopping, With Siobhan?' Is it a poem if I put it on three lines? That doesn't seem right."

"That's a very interesting point, Lucy. There has

been a trend toward looser and looser forms of poetry over the past half-century . . ."

She talks for the next thirty minutes.

"Some of the most noted poets of our day say we need to get back to discipline and structure. George Bowering, who was Canada's first Poet Laureate, said. . . ."

We never get to hear what he said. The bell rings.

For the first time in my life, it's me who turns to look at Brandy. I give her a wink. What if she hauls off and punches me? She doesn't. She winks back.

I have just messed up a whole class so she doesn't have to do her book report. Should I feel guilty? I don't.

Friday night we're just finishing dinner when we hear a car pull up outside our trailer. I look out the window. It isn't Gina. The dog starts barking. Mom goes to the door. The dog rushes out to sniff the shoes and ankles of the two men standing on our little porch. They are wearing casual clothes, but one of them flashes a badge.

"RCMP," he says.

Mom's face falls. "Is something wrong? My parents? Harold?"

"Oh no, ma'am, nothing like that. We'd just like to talk to you, if you don't mind."

Mom steps back from the door. "Come on in."

No one sits down. The three of them just stand there. I'm back by the cupboards, watching.

"It's about your shed, ma'am."

"What about the shed?" she says.

"We've had a complaint."

Mom spins around. "Lucy, did you . . . ?"

I shake my head no.

"Would you mind if we checked it out?" the bigger of the two guys asks.

"*I* don't care, but I can't let you in. I don't have the key."

"And who would have it?" asks the other fellow.

"My landlord, Randy."

The larger cop takes out a notebook and writes something down. "Does this Randy have a last name?"

"Larson," she says.

"And where does he live?"

"Just two trailers down, on the other side of the road here. Lucy, why don't you go see if he's home."

"It's just a padlock," I tell them. "You could break in pretty easily, I think."

I've seen these things on TV.

"We don't have a warrant," says the smaller guy. "We were just hoping you'd want to cooperate. Our informant didn't think you were involved."

"Involved in what?" Mom asks.

She can be so naive!

"The informant suspects there might be a small marijuana grow-op in the shed. Says she hears humming noises and that you complain that your hydro bill is very high."

Mom glares at me again. I just shrug. I think we both have a pretty good idea of who the informant is.

"Do you want me to go see if Randy's home?" I ask the officer.

"No, I don't think that would be wise. Thanks for your help. We'll just wait outside here till there's another officer available to talk to this Randy."

They walk out and get back into the dark blue Chevy Caprice they've parked in front of our trailer. We watch them through the window. One of them is talking on their radio. They don't start the car.

Mom grabs the phone and looks in her address book for a number. Her hands are shaking a bit as she punches it in.

"Randy, what have you got in that shed?" she asks.

There's a pause.

"Well, I've got two police officers in my driveway, and I think they just called for backup."

There's another little pause, and then she hangs up without saying good-bye.

"He's coming over."

A police cruiser pulls in behind the Caprice. The two officers in this car are in uniform. Randy walks up just as they're getting out. He's talking to them, but I can't hear what anyone is saying. I step onto the little porch. The dog is barking like crazy. This is way too much excitement for her.

A third car pulls up. We have a traffic jam in front of our trailer. A woman gets out and comes up the steps toward me.

"Are you Lucy?" she asks.

"Yes." Who could this be, and how does she know my name?

Mom has stepped outside and is right behind me.

"Mrs. Jensen?" the woman asks.

"Yes."

"My name's Hilda Thompson. I'm a social worker with the Ministry of Children and Families." She hands Mom her card.

Randy and the four police officers have gone around to the other side of the shed.

"We've had a report that your daughter may be in a dangerous situation, and I've been sent to investigate. I'll want to talk to you too, of course. But first I'd like to speak to Lucy alone."

My mother is looking totally shell-shocked.

The social worker turns to where the police are still gathered at the end of our lean-to and says, "I wonder if Lucy really needs to see all this. Maybe it would be better if I took her back to my office. You and I can talk after you're finished with the police here." Then she turns to me. "Would you be comfortable with that, Lucy?"

"I guess so." Actually, I'd rather stay and see what happens here, but I don't want her to think I'm just a snoop.

"Would that be okay with you, Mrs. Jensen?"

Mom looks at the business card the worker gave her. "Your office is on Guildford Way?"

"Yes. There's a bit of a strip mall there."

"And when do you think you'll get back to me?"

"Oh, it shouldn't be more than an hour."

Mom nods. "Okay," she says. She's still standing there, looking at the business card, when we drive off.

Ms. Thompson doesn't say much while we're driving to her office. It gives me time to think. If she decides that I'm not safe at my mom's house, I won't have to live there. And I already know that my dad can't look after me because he works such long hours. They might send me to a foster home. If I could get into that group home on Siobhan's street, I'd be able to see her every day. Of course, I'd miss my mom, and she'd be heartbroken if I was taken away. But I'm sure she'd visit me every single day – even if it is a long drive. When I'm in Langley, I'm lucky if I see Siobhan once a week. And Siobhan is making new friends. My mom isn't going to get a new daughter just because I'm not around as much as usual. I'd never have thought of a plan like this myself, but God has let it fall right into my lap. I guess He's listening after all.

When we get to the office, Ms. Thompson takes me to a room that has a sofa and an easy chair in it. There's a fridge in the corner.

"Would you like a soft drink?" she asks.

"Yes, please."

When I'm comfortable, she sits down and starts asking me questions.

"Do you know why the police were at your home this evening?"

"I'm assuming it was Mrs. Warren who called them," I say.

"What makes you think that?"

"Well, I've suspected there might be marijuana growing in that shed, and I told my mom about it, but she said I should just mind my own business."

"So did you tell anyone else your worries?"

"Just Mrs. Warren. That's why I think it must have been her who called the police. The thing is, I'm on my own a lot – what with my mom working and then going out on dates or to nightclubs – and I didn't like having that Randy lurking around our trailer."

Ms. Thompson is taking notes like mad.

"Mom even complained that our hydro bill was as high for that little trailer as it had been for our house, which was over three thousand square feet. You have to worry about the fire hazard too, if he's got such big lights in such a small shed."

"What is your mother's relationship with this Randy?" Mrs. Thompson asks.

"He's our landlord."

"Does your mom have a social relationship with him as well?" she asks.

"Well, he came to a party she had at our house once."

"But they aren't dating or anything like that," she says.

"No, it's Randy's roommate, Jake, she dated." I'm trying to think of whether there's anything else I can say to convince her I should go to a foster home. "Mrs. Warren almost called the police once before," I say. "There's a girl who lives in our trailer park who has been bullying me. She was about to beat me up, and Mrs. Warren came out with her phone and said she was calling the police. That scared Brandy off."

"Where was your mother when that happened?"

"She was still at work. Mrs. Warren didn't think it was safe for me to be in our trailer on my own, so I stayed at her place till my mom got home."

When Ms. Thompson is finished asking me questions, she asks if there is somewhere other than my mom's place that I could spend the night.

"There's a foster home on One-hundred-and-eighteenth Street that just started up. They only take teenage girls, and they can have up to three. I happen to know they only have one right now."

"Do you know someone who lives there?" she asks.

"No, but my best friend, Siobhan, lives just two doors down, and she told me all about it."

"I'll just call your mom and see if she has any other suggestions," she says.

Why ask her?

But Ms. Thompson does ask, and when she comes back, she tells me that Grandma will be picking me up.

I expect Grandma to be really mad at Mom, but she isn't talking about it. She's just generally crabby. She doesn't even ask me what happened. She's only interested in finishing her packing. She and Granddad are leaving for Las Vegas tomorrow. They're going with Fred and Muriel, a woman Grandma met at her bridge club. Grandma and Granddad went to the casino with them too. I don't really think it is appropriate for old people to be hanging around casinos, but still I'm glad Grandma and Granddad are going away. When they leave, the social worker will have to send me to that foster home.

I don't care if Grandma wants to ignore me. I know Siobhan will be totally blown away when she hears my story. I call her right away, even though it's getting pretty late.

"Two patrol cars?" she says. "Your mom must have been so embarrassed. Did they have their red and blues flashing and everything?"

"No. Actually, the first officers who came weren't even in a police car."

"Oh, it was a police car, I'm sure," Siobhan says. "Some of them are unmarked so they can take people by surprise."

"So did they handcuff Randy?"

"I had to leave before then, but I imagine they'd have to do that before they put him in the cop car. Did I tell you that the marked police car had that grating between the front and back seats so they could haul away the criminals?"

"What was the social worker like?"

"Quite nice. I told her I wanted to go to the foster home Megan is in."

"That would be so cool! But Megan won't be there. Didn't I tell you that her dad's coming to take her back to Saskatchewan?"

Well, that's a relief.

"That's okay," I say. "I just wanted to go there because it's so close to your place."

"But then why are you at your grandma's?"

"It's just temporary. I'm just here while Ms. Thompson is finishing her investigation. Grandma and Granddad are leaving for Las Vegas tomorrow. I might spend the weekend with my dad, so I probably won't get into the foster home till Monday."

It's not long before I am totally disappointed. Mom calls Grandma's house and says they've sorted everything out and I can come home.

"But did Ms. Thompson say I could?" I ask.

"Yeah, she's finished her investigation."

"But I read that it isn't safe to live in a house where there's been a grow-op. There's mold and stuff, and then half the time they've done weird things to the wiring so it's a fire hazard. I think I should stay in a foster home, at least till everything has been checked out."

"Lucy," she says, "it's been checked out. The humming you heard was Randy's deepfreeze."

"But what about the big hydro bills?"

"He had one salmon and a couple of pounds of freezer-burned hamburger meat in there. That was all. It was a full-size freezer, and when there's so little inside, it really uses a lot of power."

"So he wasn't charged with anything?"

"Last I heard, it wasn't illegal to leave an almost empty freezer plugged in. Anyway, he's unplugged the freezer and taken his meat over to Jake's so it's probably safe for you to come home."

I feel like an idiot.

"You must be about ready for bed now."

I am.

"Let me talk to Grandma."

After she talks to Grandma, she wants to talk to me again.

"I'm going to look at a house tomorrow morning, but Grandma says you can stay there tonight. I'll pick you up around three tomorrow afternoon."

"What about Dad? It's the weekend. I should be going to his place."

"He's busy too. He says he'll pick you up from here around five."

Do I get any choice about any of this? No way. You'd think I was a piece of baggage. "And who's looking after the dog?" I ask.

"She's fine," Mom says. "I'll walk her before I go out tomorrow, and she'll be with me when I come to get you."

And I suppose I have to be satisfied with that, though it turns out that that is not what happens at all.

The next morning, I'm sitting there eating cereal in front of the TV (I would not be allowed to do this at home) when the phone rings.

It's Muriel. I can only hear Grandma's half of the conversation, but it sounds like there's some kind of problem. There is. It's me. Muriel wants to leave early. The bus they're catching from Vancouver to the casino doesn't leave until late afternoon, but she and Fred forgot that their son has their camera. They want to pick it up at his house in Vancouver first. Muriel thinks that if they are going in early anyway, they might as well go out for dim sum. I hear Grandma telling Granddad about it.

"Well, call Kate," he says. "She'll just have to take Lucy with her."

I don't wait for them to call. I know when I'm not wanted. I call Mom to see if she can come and get me early. I get no answer. It doesn't matter. It's not like I've never been left by myself before. I tell Granddad and Grandma they should go ahead and meet their friends as long as they don't mind taking me home first. Grandma's all apologetic, but while she's apologizing, Granddad is loading their suitcases into the car and he tosses my backpack in on top of them. The matter is decided.

It's not quite nine o'clock when they drop me off at our trailer. Mom's car is there, but things look pretty dead. She's probably still asleep, so Grandma doesn't come in.

The dog comes pitter-pattering out from my bedroom. I pick her up and give her a cuddle. I take her for a little bit of a walk. It's not until I come in the second time that I notice the pair of men's running shoes placed neatly behind the door. They're white with silver markings, and there's a small, royal blue crescent-shaped logo on the side. The lining of the shoes is the same royal blue. I look around the place. I can't see any clues as to who they might belong to. I creep down the hall. I stop outside Mom's bedroom door and listen. I hear heavy breathing. My mom is a light breather. Someone with a deep voice gives a small cough. My mom is not alone in there. She has a man in her bed.

She's the one sleeping around, so why am I so embarrassed? I sneak back out of the trailer. If she caught me catching her, I'd just die. How could she do this?

I start out toward the entrance to the trailer park. As I pass Jake's trailer, I see his car's there. It makes sense; he'd hardly bother to drive over to our trailer. I wonder if she changed her sheets. He probably wouldn't even care.

I don't know where to go. Grandma's on her way to Las Vegas. I don't want my dad knowing Mom's in bed with some guy. That leaves Siobhan. Her mother's not going to drive all the way to Langley to get me, but if I just turn up on their doorstep, she's not so hard-hearted that she'd just throw me out.

I'll have to get there on my own. I check my wallet. I have five dollars. There's a bus stop just down the street from the entrance to the trailer park. The trouble is that this time I don't have a trip plan from the bus company's Web site to guide me.

I wait until a bus pulls up, and then I stick my head through the door and ask if this bus will get me to Surrey.

"Well, not directly," he answers. "Where in Surrey are you going?"

"Scott Road and Eighty-sixth Avenue," I say.

"You'll need to make a few transfers, but you should start with the C61 to Langley Centre."

The bus pulls away. I stand there waiting for the C61. It arrives and I get on. At least this time, the bus isn't crowded and there are lots of seats. I remember to ask for a transfer.

"I'm trying to get to Surrey, to Scott Road and Eighty-sixth Avenue. Which bus should I take after this one?"

The driver hems and hahs but finally suggests I try the one to Surrey Central.

Three buses and two-and-a-half hours later, I get to Siobhan's. And people wonder why we have gridlock on our highways. Why would anyone ever take a bus if it always takes four or five times longer than it would by car? I can't wait to be old enough to drive and add my share to the pollution.

Siobhan is totally surprised to see me, but at least she's home and not out somewhere with Megan. Her mother is unpacking groceries, and all the kids are hanging around, whining or fighting.

"Can I go out now?" she asks her mom. "Lucy and I want to go down to the mall."

Actually, I don't want to go to the mall at all, but what are the choices? I can't talk to her here, with her mom and all these kids listening.

"I don't have any money," I say.

"Like, what's new? We never have any money. But guess what?"

I can't guess.

"All that's going to change! I've got a real babysitting job for next Saturday."

I don't know why she'd be excited about a babysitting job. She's always babysitting, and I don't even think she likes it.

"Five dollars an hour and they only have two kids. Sure beats being treated like slave labor."

Siobhan's mother rolls her eyes and reaches for her purse. "Well, I can't compete with wages like that, but you have to consider that I do provide you with free room and board." She hands Siobhan a ten dollar bill. "Don't spend it all in one place. And that's for tonight too, so don't get any funny ideas now that you're in demand."

"Maybe Lucy could stay over and help me with the kids tonight," Siobhan says.

She makes it sound like this is something I'd be dying to do. Still, it would better than having to face my mom or dad.

"I'd have to ask my mom," I say.

"You can use the phone in my room," Siobhan says.

I'm praying Mom is home because otherwise she's going to turn up looking for me at Grandma's in an hour or two. I'm in luck. She says she was just heading out to go grocery shopping. I tell her Grandma and Granddad left early, and I'm at Siobhan's. She doesn't ask how I got there. She says I can stay over if it's okay with Siobhan's mom, which it is.

On our way to the mall, I tell Siobhan about what I walked in on this morning. "You have no idea how sleazy it feels," I say, "knowing your own mother is in bed with some guy just a few feet away from where you're standing."

"And you were standing with your ear right up to the door?"

"Right. I'm absolutely sure it was a man's breathing and a man's cough . . . I mean, I'd have known anyway, what with the shoes out there by the door."

"So you think it's that Jake?"

"That's what I'm assuming. There was no other car. He lives close enough to walk over."

"Or maybe it's Randy. He lives in the same place, doesn't he?"

"I didn't think of him," I say.

We're so wrapped up in our conversation we don't even bother to go shopping. We just go into one of the coffee shops and order colas and fries.

"You know, just because there was no other car there doesn't mean it had to be someone who lived close enough to walk," Siobhan says as soon as the server walks away to fill our order.

"How else would he have got there?"

"Well, if your mom met someone at a club or at the pub, she might have just brought him home. Especially if one of them had been drinking too much. They'd just leave their car at the bar overnight."

I think about it. I suppose she's right. Sometimes when I'm feeling bad about things, Siobhan is a really good friend to have. She can completely take my mind off my troubles. This isn't one of those times. It felt bad enough when I thought Mom was in bed with Jake, but that's not as bad as thinking maybe she picked up some stranger when one or both of them was too drunk to drive.

"I have no idea what's got into her," I say.

"This has been a really exciting month for your mom. You know, first she got accepted for that course, so she knows she'll be quitting her prissy old job at the convent. And now your parents have sold the house, so she'll have all this money and she can do whatever she wants with it. Maybe she just wants to make a fresh start and be like a totally different sort of person. She's only twenty-eight. She's still got time to change if she wants to."

I feel like kicking Siobhan. Maybe because she's just said exactly what I've been thinking. I wish I'd said it. And I wish that when I did, Siobhan had told me I was crazy.

Instead, all I say is, "She's twenty-nine next week. I get tired of hearing how young she is. I'll be glad when she's thirty."

I've babysat with Siobhan before. It's not too bad if her parents don't go out until seven o'clock or so, like tonight. Her mom's got the little ones in bed already. Rebecca and

Jasmine, who are a bit older, are bathed and in their pj's. Their mom has told them they can watch one show. Kevin and Damien are the most trouble. They're nine and twelve. They hate it that Siobhan gets to be the boss of them. They never want to do what she says.

Just as her dad is getting into his jacket, Siobhan says, "Dad, tell Kevin and Damien what time they have to go to bed. I don't want to spend all night fighting with them."

"Damien, Kevin, Nine-thirty. Got it? I don't want to hear that you've given Siobhan a hard time or there will be consequences. Understand?"

Damien and Kevin scowl at Siobhan, but they nod their heads. Then they disappear down the stairs to the basement to play some video game. Siobhan goes into the kitchen. She changes the time on the clock on the stove. Now it says eight o'clock instead of seven. Then she changes the time on the microwave, and on the alarm clock in her parents' room.

At seven-thirty, when the TV show they're watching is over, Siobhan tells Rebecca and Jasmine it's time for bed. They're pretty good about it, especially when I tell them that once they're tucked in I'll read them a story. They find the one they like. It's called *Curious George Flies a Kite*. They sure didn't pick it for the cover. The book is old, and it looks like it's been dropped in the bathtub or left out in the rain. It smells funny too. Why do they even want me to read it? They have it memorized. When I try to hurry things up a bit by skipping parts, they catch me and make me go back.

Siobhan is down checking on the boys. When I'm finished the story, she comes in and gives her sisters goodnight kisses. Then she turns out the light. We go to the kitchen and make some popcorn. We can hear the girls talking and giggling a bit, but after awhile, it's quiet.

Siobhan takes some of the popcorn to the basement for the boys.

"Nine o'clock," I hear her say. "Here's a snack. You need to get into your pajamas pretty soon."

I look at the clocks around the kitchen. Right. They all read nine o'clock.

Half an hour later, she herds them off to bed. They complain. She threatens to tell her dad. They grumble. They argue with her and with each other. I just stay out of it. There are times I'm glad I'm an only child. Finally, when all the clocks say it's ten-thirty but it's really nine-thirty, things quiet down. Siobhan goes around and changes all the clocks back.

"If I'd started trying to get them to bed when it was really nine-thirty, I'd still be fighting with them an hour later," she says. "It works better this way."

We both flop down on the couch. Siobhan had turned the TV off when she was trying to get the kids to bed, so now it seems very quiet.

"What a day. I think we deserve a drink," she says.

I agree. I don't know what she has in mind. Her family never has pop in the house. Siobhan's mom always says that water's better for us. When we get to the kitchen, Siobhan doesn't even go to the fridge. She pulls a chair up beside it, steps up on it, and begins looking through some bottles in the high cupboard over the fridge.

"Here it is," she says. "Baileys Irish Cream. I tried it at Christmas. It's not like most booze. It tastes really good."

I've never had alcohol before, but even Grandma takes a drink now and then. She says Jesus did, too. It's only a sin if you get drunk, but one glass is okay.

Siobhan steps down, opens another cupboard, and takes out glasses. She fills one for each of us. When I have mine, we wander back to the living room. We're still wondering what to do about my mom.

"She's never been the smartest about sex, has she?" asks Siobhan.

"No, I don't think she knows much about things like condoms."

"My parents neither."

I take a sip of the Irish cream drink. It's quite good. It's almost like chocolate milk, but with a little bit of a bite to it. I take a bigger drink.

"Nice, isn't it?" says Siobhan.

"Very."

She takes another sip too. "Yes," she says, "you really should have a talk with your mom."

"I'd be too embarrassed. I don't even want her to know that I know."

"I know it will be hard, but if she's already bringing guys home to spend the night, she needs to be using some kind of protection."

We talk about it for quite awhile. Siobhan thinks maybe I could print out something about condoms from the Internet and just leave it where Mom would find it. I'm more interested in finding some way to persuade Mom not to sleep with these guys at all. How do I try to talk her out of being a floozy without telling her I know she's been acting like one?

"I guess I'll have to . . ." I start.

I've only drunk about two-thirds of my Irish Cream, but I'm feeling odd: queasy and funny in the head.

Siobhan takes another big swallow from her glass. "It's probably too late to talk to her about just saying no," she says.

I get up to go to the bathroom. "Excuse me. I'll be back in a minute."

I'm a bit dizzy. I bump into the coffee table. When I get to the bathroom, I go to hit the light switch, but I miss it. It takes me two or three tries. Mind you, it is dark, but I don't think I usually have any trouble. My stomach feels awful. I'm trying to think of what I ate today. Pretty soon I know. I barely make it to the toilet, and I hurl; it looks like popcorn mostly. It takes me by surprise. I didn't get the seat up. It's splattered all over. I take some toilet paper, and I'm down on my knees in front of the bowl, trying to clean up, when it hits me again.

This is so totally gross. I'm here on my knees, hanging on to the sides of someone else's toilet. Where is my mother when I need her? I've got it on my shirt. I pull myself up to the sink and use a washcloth to try to clean it off. The smell of the puke makes me gag. I barely make it to the toilet again. The sweat is pouring off me. I just sit there on the floor for awhile, leaning against the wall next to the toilet. I don't know how long I'm there. I'm starting to feel a little bit better, so, being careful not to make any sudden moves, I start trying to clean up the mess I've made.

Siobhan must think I've died in here. I'm surprised she hasn't come to check on me. I wash my face. I look at myself in the mirror. I'm awfully pale. Maybe I'm coming down with something. That Irish Cream probably didn't help any.

When I think I'm okay, I come out of the bathroom and walk back down the hall. I bump into the walls a couple of times, but I don't have any major problems. When I get to the living room, I see why Siobhan hasn't come to check on me. She's sound asleep on the couch. Our dirty glasses are sitting there. Both of them are empty. I thought I'd left some in mine. Whatever. I take them to the kitchen and put them in the dishwasher. I tidy up a bit, even though I'm still kind of clumsy and keep bumping into things. It's eleven o'clock. Siobhan's mom and dad will be home pretty soon. We should be getting ready for bed ourselves. I really need some sleep. I'm so tired I can't think straight.

"Siobhan, wake up. Time for bed." I give her shoulder a little shake.

Then I laugh at myself. That sounds weird, telling someone to wake up because it's time for bed.

"Siobhan!" I say it louder this time, and I give her shoulder a harder shake.

She doesn't even open her eyes. She's breathing slowly, like she's in a really deep sleep. At least she's breathing. Why won't she wake up? I grab her by both shoulders and shake her hard, yelling at her to wake up. Her eyelids flicker, but she just drops back into the corner of the couch like a rag doll when I let her go. Water! Maybe I should throw a glass of cold water on her. It would get on the couch. Her mother would have a fit. I run to the kitchen and soak a dish towel with cold water. I'm coming back to put it on her face when I hear the car in the driveway.

I wipe her face down and pinch her hard on the soft part of her inner arm.

"You girls still up?" I hear her dad ask.

Then both he and her mom are standing there, looking at us.

"I can't get her to wake up," I say. "She's breathing and everything, but she won't wake up."

Siobhan's dad is standing over her. He half lifts her off the couch and shakes her hard. Her eyes flutter and she makes a bit of a grunt, but that's it. Her head lolls on her chest. If he let go, she'd fall in a heap on the floor.

"I'll call 911," Siobhan's mom says.

"Never mind," her dad says. "I'll carry her to the car. It will be faster than waiting for an ambulance."

Siobhan's mother bends over Siobhan so she can

help carry her. She sniffs. "Liam, she's been drinking. I can smell it." She looks at me. "What have the two of you been in to?"

"We just had a glass of that Irish Cream."

They're walking toward the front door. They each have Siobhan under one arm. Her feet are dragging along the carpet. The bathroom is just two doors down the hall.

Siobhan's mom sniffs again. "Who's been puking? Has she been sick too? I can smell it."

"No," I say. "That was me. Siobhan wasn't sick, but now she won't wake up."

I'm following them, and I misjudge where the railing is and bump into it.

Siobhan's mom looks like she's going to cry. "You're not in much better shape than she is."

They get her downstairs and out to the car. I'm following them. I don't have a jacket on; I'm shivering. Siobhan's dad gets her into the front seat, and her mom leans over from the driver's side to fasten Siobhan's seat belt.

"She won't wake up," I say.

Siobhan's dad looks at me but says to Colleen, "You better take this one too. If she's been as sick as she smells, she should at least be checked out."

He gets me into the backseat and helps me with my seat belt. Siobhan's mom has started the engine.

"Don't worry 'bout me," I say. "The thing is, Siobhan won't . . ."

"Shut up, Lucy. I know she won't wake up. You've told me about twenty times," Siobhan's mom says.

Her dad goes back into the house and we drive away. I must fall asleep.

twenty

Next thing I know, there are lights all around me. Someone's taking Siobhan out of the front seat. Someone is saying my name, asking me questions. It's a strange woman, and she undoes my seat belt and helps me out of the car. There's a wheelchair there, and she guides me into it. We're at the emergency department of the hospital. They've already taken Siobhan in. They leave me in the waiting room, but Siobhan and her mom go into another room where there are beds with curtains around them.

Is she going to be okay? Why would she be unconscious? There's no one here to ask, just some guy holding a bloody cloth to his head and a lady with a baby who is fussing and coughing.

The entrance we came through has big double doors that open automatically. Now they open again, and my mom and dad come in together. They see me right away, which isn't hard because, like I say, there's hardly anyone else in the waiting room. Mom comes running over and kneels down by the wheelchair so her head's even with mine.

"Are you all right?" she asks. "Have they checked you yet?"

I shake my head no.

"How do you feel?" Dad asks.

"Not wonderful," I say. "But, Dad, Siobhan won't wake up. She's unconscious." The tears start to come. At first they just slide down my cheeks while I'm trying to talk. "What if she dies?"

Mom puts her arms around me. I don't know how she stands it because I know I smell very bad. Somehow it makes me cry harder. Dad goes and answers some questions so the nurse at the front desk can fill out a form. I calm myself down a bit so that when another nurse comes to get me I can at least talk to her.

She wheels me into a small office. She takes my blood pressure and my temperature. All the time she's asking me questions.

"What were you drinking?"

"Irish Cream," I answer.

"And how much did you have?"

"About three-quarters of a glass."

"What about your friend, was she drinking the same thing?"

I nod.

"Did she have the same amount you had?"

"A little more," I tell her. "We started out with the same, but I started feeling sick so I went to the bathroom. When I came back, Siobhan's drink was gone and so was mine. I think she finished both of them."

"Did you take any acetaminophen or other pills?"

"No."

"Did you use any other drugs at all: marijuana, cocaine, ecstasy . . ."

"Of course not!" I say. What kind of a kid does she think I am?

A doctor comes in. He checks my eyes with a light. He reads the notes that the nurse took. Then he turns to my mom. "She probably got rid of most of it when she vomited," he says. "Looks like you just have a drunk on your hands. She'll be hung over tomorrow, but other than that, she'll be fine."

He folds up his stethoscope and walks away like he's got more important things to do, which he probably has.

I'm mortified.

"He thinks I'm a drunk," I say.

Mom just raises her eyebrows at me. She probably thinks I'm a drunk too.

When we get back to the waiting room, Siobhan's mom is there. Right away she comes up to my mom and puts her arms around her. "I'm so sorry," she says. "And I criticized you for not supervising properly. I'm such a hypocrite."

Mom returns her hug. "Never mind that now. How's Siobhan?"

"Will she be okay?" I ask. I can feel the tears coming again.

"We got her here in time. She'll be fine, but they're going to keep her overnight to be sure. They've got her on an IV. Something about electrolytes."

Siobhan's mom's been crying. She sniffles. Mom gets a tissue from her purse and hands it to her.

"I never thought they'd do something like this," Siobhan's mom says.

"Well, Siobhan's fourteen and Lucy will be too, come November. We've all been warned about that age," Mom says.

What does she mean by that?

I fall asleep on the way home to the trailer park. Next thing I remember is Dad lifting me out of the van. Then I'm in my own bed and the dog is curled up beside me.

I don't feel too good when I wake up the next morning. The dog is gone. I look at my clock. It's after ten. We always go to ten-thirty mass. I'm never going to make it. Why didn't Mom wake me up? I jump out of bed and wish I hadn't. The world spins for a minute. My stomach lurches. I lie down again. It's too late to make it to church anyway.

I try to sleep some more. Usually when I'm sick, I sleep a lot, but this time I can't. Finally, after half an hour of trying, I get up again, but very slowly. I really need to get something to drink. I wander into the kitchen in my nightshirt. The place is so quiet I'm thinking Mom has gone to mass without me. She hasn't. She's sitting on the couch, drinking coffee.

"Ah!" she says when she sees me. "Our invalid. I think some juice would probably be in order."

She pours me a big glass of orange juice from the fridge. I sit down on the chair opposite her and take a couple of gulps.

"Feeling rough?" she asks.

I nod; it hurts my head.

"Colleen called. They picked Siobhan up this morning. She's fine."

I'm so relieved, but then, like an idiot, I start crying again. "I was so afraid. I thought there was something seriously wrong with her."

"It *was* serious," Mom says. "She had alcohol poisoning. People can die from that."

My glass is empty. Mom pours the last of the orange juice into it and takes the empty jug over to the sink.

"But we only had one drink; even Grandma says one drink is okay."

"And did Grandma say you should help yourself to one anytime you wanted?"

"No." I can't meet her eyes. I look down at the table in front of me. There's a section of the newspaper there. It's open to the crossword puzzle, and I notice it has all been filled in. No blanks spaces left this time.

"And how big was the one drink you had, Lucy?"

"Just a regular glass, like this one." I hold up my juice glass to show her.

"Irish Cream is a liqueur. There's as much alcohol in one ounce of it as there would be in a whole bottle of beer. It's usually served in tiny little glasses."

"So what we drank would be like eight or ten bottles of beer?"

She nods. "And you probably drank it fast too."

"We didn't drink any faster than we usually do," I say.

"Yeah, but usually you're drinking water or milk, not alcohol."

How does she know all this stuff anyway?

"Did something like this ever happen to you when you were younger?" I'm sort of hoping she'll say yes. Maybe then I wouldn't feel like such a loser. I cringe every time I think of that doctor calling me a drunk.

"No."

"How come you know so much about it?"

"I've read about it, seen it on TV."

That's how I know about condoms. So now I'm thinking maybe Mom's heard about them too. I hope so. She could still get pregnant even if she is almost thirty. And with her maybe picking up strange men in bars, she needs to be thinking about AIDS and those other diseases you can get from sex.

"You could sure use a shower," she says.

She reaches across and touches a piece of my hair. It's crunchy. I have puke in my hair. Gross.

When I've had a shower and washed my hair, I go into my room and flop down on my bed. The dog comes in and grunts until I lift her up beside me. I lie there, staring at the ceiling for awhile. I'm still thinking about Mom.

Maybe she wouldn't use a condom because she's Catholic and we're not supposed to. Of course, she shouldn't be sleeping with men she's not married to either. Adultery is a mortal sin. I'm not sure if using a condom when you're already committing a mortal sin makes it a worse sin or not. It seems to me, if she can avoid getting a horrible disease, she'll live longer and have more time to repent. That would be good. It's all too complicated. It makes my head hurt thinking about it.

I wish I could sleep some more, but I keep tossing and turning, thinking about sin – which reminds me, I missed mass this morning. That's a mortal sin too. So is getting drunk. I'm in big trouble with God.

There's a knock at the trailer door. The dog barks and jumps down to go investigate. Then I hear my dad's voice. I don't know what he's doing here. Probably checking up on his hungover drunk of a daughter. I pull on a pair of jeans and a T-shirt.

I walk down the hall, and the first thing I see is a pair of men's running shoes on the mat by the door. They're white with silver markings and there's a small royal blue crescent-shaped logo on the side. The inside of the shoes is the same royal blue. I stop for a minute and stare at them. Dad's sitting at the kitchen table with Mom, spreading out some tile samples.

"Where did you get those shoes?" I ask him.

"Walmart. $69.95."

"When?"

He stops what he's doing and looks at me. "A week or so ago. Why?"

I just give a shrug.

"We have some things to discuss with you," he says.

"You girls really let us down last night," Mom says. "We expected better than that from you."

"We had a talk with Siobhan's parents this morning," Dad says. "They're grounding Siobhan for two weeks. She won't be allowed to visit or talk to anyone on the phone."

"So go ahead and ground me too," I say.

If Siobhan is grounded, there's no one for me to phone or visit anyway.

Mom and Dad exchange a look.

"I think that would be just too easy for you," Dad says. "We've decided we're going to put you to work."

"Where? What do you mean?"

"You're going to have some extra chores to do," Mom says.

I look around the trailer. There's not much to do here, even if Mom were to go on strike completely. How bad could it be? But that isn't what they have in mind.

They put me to work in the backyard of the house Dad has bought. It's not very large, but there's a tall fence all around it, so the dog comes along to keep me company. She thinks it's a great adventure because the plants and grass are way over her head. I keep thinking I've lost her. At one time, there was a vegetable garden in one part of the yard. That's what I'm supposed to work on. Who needs broccoli plants three feet high, especially when they're from last year? I spend all of Monday evening pulling up big old vegetables.

Dad's taken vacation time to work on the house. It's a good break for him now that tax time is over. He picked me up right after school and brought me here. Mom comes by later with a pot of chili, and we eat dinner together. She's wearing her grungiest work clothes, and, after dinner, she starts pouring paint into a tray.

"What are you doing?" I ask. She didn't get drunk. She didn't even sleep with Jake. Why is she sharing my punishment?

"I'm starting on the bedrooms," she answers.

"Why are you painting Dad's house?"

"Because it's my house too," she says. "This was the house I wanted to look at on Saturday morning. Your dad and I are going halfers on it."

This makes no sense. "So who's going to live here?" I ask.

"You and me," Mom says.

"I thought you didn't want to rent from Dad."

"But I'm not. I put some money into the house too, and I'm the one who'll pay the mortgage."

"We're going to fix it up, and, in a couple of years, when your mom is finished her course, we'll be able to sell it and make a tidy profit," Dad says.

"So you're business partners?"

They smile a bit at each other.

"You could put it that way," Mom says.

Yeah. Business partners who ended up sleeping together on Friday night.

I work on the house every night that week. I even learn how to use a weed trimmer. By the time I finish cutting the long grass in about a quarter of the backyard, my hands are shaking so badly I can't drink a glass of water without spilling it. I'm sure the vibration from that machine has caused some sort of weird nerve damage. I want Mom to take me to the emergency room, but she says it's nothing to worry about and that it will go away on its own.

She's having a break too. "You realize this house is only a five-minute drive from Siobhan's?" she asks.

Like she thinks I wouldn't notice.

"You two will be able to catch the bus to Holy Name together."

"I know," I say. "I've been counting on it."

"Once my course starts, I'll have to leave way too early to drive you, but I'm sure Grandma wouldn't mind . . ."

"Oh, let's not bother Grandma," I say. "If I can get a bus from Holy Name to Langley, I can easily take one from here to Siobhan's."

I've already looked it up. One bus, five minutes. Maybe ten if I add a bit of a walk on each end.

"That would be great," Mom says. "I think Grandma

has a lot of other interests these days. What do you think about all this gambling she's doing?"

"I really don't approve. Do you think that Muriel is a bad influence?"

"Well, I wondered if it was Granddad who was leading her astray."

We don't get any more work done that night. We're too busy discussing Grandma.

Acknowledgements

I owe a debt of gratitude to my good friends Jean Bullard and Bonnie Lepin who read earlier drafts of this story and offered their suggestions and encouragement. Thanks too, to Tundra publisher, Kathy Lowinger, who took the time to give me some lessons in plotting and to Kelly Jones and Kathryn Cole for asking all the right questions and helping me say what I meant to say all along.

This book would never have made it as far as an editor's desk had Bill Richardson not offered his encouragement and persuaded his friend Carolyn Swayze to act as my agent. Finally, a big thanks to Carolyn for her quiet persistence and faith in me and in this book.